Praise for

THE DROWNED BOY

"Karin Fossum's minimalist police procedurals featuring her Norwegian detective, Inspector Konrad Sejer, have a stealthy way of mutating into richer, if also darker, psychological studies of criminals and their victims . . . In the end, the novel isn't about willful murder or even accidental death, but the psychological aftershocks for the living." — *New York Times Book Review*

"Sejer asks himself, 'if this really was a murder case,' could the crime be proven if there weren't any witnesses? The answer, in this sensitive and shocking work, comes as unexpectedly as the punch line in a shaggy-dog story—and with the same off-kilter cosmic logic." — *Wall Street Journal*

"Simple but gripping story, balanced, believable and compassionate, about a sensitive subject." — *Guardian*

"Karin Fossum is regarded as the queen of crime fiction and with *The Drowned Boy* she proves just what a powerful writer she is . . . An excellent book that will stay with you for a very long time. It concludes with a twist of fate that is as bizarre as it is delightful." — *Crime Fiction Lover*

"The ending of the book cannot be revealed without ruining its impact, but it is the kind of quiet, cold climax to be expected from Ms. Fossum, and she does not disappoint."

— *Washington Times*

"Compelling work from the author who seems to have inherited the late Ruth Rendell's gift of spinning the darkest complications out of what might seem like nothing at all." — *Kirkus Reviews*

"The real strength of the book lies in the characters Fossum has crafted. Sejer is not the typical unhappy, unhealthy Scandinavian detective; instead, he's a widower who is kind to his suspects and colleagues alike . . . Fossum's twelfth Sejer installment doesn't disappoint. Her writing style keeps the reader guessing to the final page. This title will appeal to mystery readers of all stripes."

— *Library Journal*

"Powerful and disturbing . . . A riveting tale that's more psychological study than police procedural."

— *Publishers Weekly*, starred review

"A chilling crime novel from the award-winning Fossum."

— *Booklist*, starred review

THE DROWNED BOY

Also by Karin Fossum

The
Drowned Boy

....

Karin Fossum

Translated from the Norwegian
by Kari Dickson

Mariner Books
Houghton Mifflin Harcourt
BOSTON • NEW YORK

First Mariner Books edition 2016

For information about permission to reproduce selections from this
book, write to trade.permissions@hmhco.com or to Permissions,
Houghton Mifflin Harcourt Publishing Company,
3 Park Avenue, 19th Floor, New York, New York 10016.

First published with the title *Carmen Zita og døden* in Norway by
Cappelen Damm in 2013

First published in Great Britain in 2015 by Harvill Secker

www.hmhco.com

Library of Congress Cataloging-in-Publication Data
Fossum, Karin, date, author.
[Carmen Zita og døden. English]
The drowned boy / Karin Fossum.
pages cm
ISBN 978-0-544-48396-5 (hardback)—
ISBN 978-0-544-70484-8 (paperback)—ISBN 978-0-544-43355-7 (ebook)
1. Murder—Investigation—Fiction. I. Title.
PT8951.16.0735C3713 2015
839.823'8—dc23
2015015904

Printed in the United States of America
DOC 10 9 8 7 6 5 4 3 2 1

THE DROWNED BOY

Why does my child have the eyes of a fish
and the claws of a bird?

Prologue

IF A VICTIM falls into water unexpectedly, he will immediately take one or two deep breaths (respiration surprise) and thus draw water down into the airways, which triggers violent and sustained coughing. When the victim is then wholly immersed in water, he holds his breath and will in most cases float up to the surface again. Whereupon he will gasp for air and once more draw water down into his lungs, thus causing further coughing. The drowning person is then overcome by panic and will scream and thrash with his arms and legs, splashing around on the surface, grabbing hold of anything within reach: a boat, an oar, a friend.

The head is immersed again and more water is drawn down into the lungs in deep breaths. The victim may float back up to the surface once or several times more, but not necessarily three as folklore would lead us to believe. Finally he sinks to the bottom and all is over. This struggle in the water can last for just under a minute or several minutes, depending on the physical health and general stamina of the victim. But eventually he will sink to the bottom, exhausted, open his mouth, and draw the water down into his lungs. He will lose consciousness, go into spasms, and start retching; he will turn blue and become limp. And finally, following this fierce fight for life, he will fall into a coma and die.

1

THE DIZZINESS HIT him in short, sharp bursts that overwhelmed him. Even though he fought against it, he lost his balance. This is not good, he thought to himself in desperation. This is it. He tried as best he could to stay on his feet, managing somehow to get over to the mirror on the wall to study his face with keen eyes. No, I can't ignore it anymore. It must be a tumor, he thought, presumably a brain tumor. Why should I get away with it? I'm no better than anyone else, not in the slightest. Of course it was cancer. That's what we die of these days, one in three, he thought. Even one in two if we live to be old enough. And soon I'll be an old man; I'm halfway to a hundred. But I'm probably going to die now. Just like Elise died of cancer at the age of forty. Slowly, over time, she was drained of strength and became pale, jaundiced, and emaciated, with liver failure and all that goes with it. An attack of hysterical, rampant cell division as she lay in a cool white bed for those final hours in University Hospital. Stop, don't think about that now. There's enough suffering in the world.

He stood leaning against the wall for a while. Trying to breathe slowly and steadily, to gather his strength, pull himself together. Well, so be it, he thought. I can't say I wasn't prepared, because I am. I've always known it would end like this, known it for far too long. I subconsciously harbored the fear that it would get me in the end too. Like Elise. Struck down like lightning. By a virulent and aggressive disease: let's get the lungs, now the bones, and then the brain. We'll break this organism down, because that's what we do. Got to be dignified about this, he thought. Don't make a fuss—that's never good. On the other hand, it might be nothing. Please, dear God, let it be nothing. What God? he asked himself in desperation. I don't have a God, and perhaps I'm going to die. And afterward all will be dark and empty, a great nothingness, a deafening silence.

His cell phone started to ring in his pocket; despite all the chaos inside, he had to get a grip. He put the phone to his ear and heard the voice of his colleague Jacob Skarre on the other end. He sounded agitated. He was overwhelmed by another bout of dizziness. It was sudden and brutal and nearly knocked him off his feet. The cell phone fell out of his hand, so he bent down quickly to pick it up. But instead he managed to push it across the floor and under the sofa. He swore out loud and got down on his knees, then lay on his stomach and wriggled under the sofa. He spotted the phone right at the back against the baseboard. But then something caught his eye, something small and red. To his surprise, he saw that it was a Lego brick. It must have been there since Matteus was little and had managed to avoid the mop for years, a sign of sloppy work. It was a small square brick. A beautiful, completely perfect little red cube: the most versatile and beautiful brick there was, as it fit everywhere. He squeezed it in his hand and felt the sharp edges dig into his skin. And there, lying on his stomach under the sofa, childhood memories from Gamle Møllevej in Roskilde came flooding back. The white brick house with painted blue window-frames and hollyhocks by the wall, the lawn and old plum trees, and the brown speckled bantams that tripped around the lush, flowering garden. Every morning he was allowed to collect the tiny eggs in a basket. He remembered his father, stern and gray, tall and lean like himself, and his mother's porcelain figurines in the kitchen window. He snapped back and wriggled out again. He lay there for a moment, gasping for breath.

"Are you there? What happened? Did you lose your balance again?"

He muttered something unintelligible in reply, embarrassed and evasive and anxious. "It was you who called," he said brusquely. "You're the one with something to tell."

He sat up, brushed the dust from his shirt, and popped the Lego brick in his shirt pocket. The dizziness had finally subsided.

"We've got a drowning," Skarre told him. "In Damtjern, the pond up by Granfoss, you remember? About twenty minutes from Møller Church. A little boy, sixteen months old. His mother found him by the small jetty, but it was too late. The ambulance crew tried to resuscitate him for about three-quarters of an hour, to no avail. Some uncertainty as to how he ended up in the water. Also, he was naked, but we're not quite sure what that means. So pretty uncertain all around. He could of course have gotten there on his own two feet. But, well, I'm not so sure in this case. If you come over, perhaps we can sort it out. It's the last house in Dambråten, white, with a red outhouse. The boy is lying on the grass here."

"Right," he said. "I'm on my way. There in half an hour."

And then, after a short pause: "Is there something that doesn't feel right? Is that why you called?"

"Yes," Skarre replied, "it's the mother. I can't explain it, but I think we should look a bit closer. Let's just leave it at that; you know what I mean."

"Don't let people stomp all over the place," Sejer said. "Keep an eye on them. Where are the parents now?"

"At the station," Skarre informed him. "Holthemann is looking after them. The mother is hysterical and the father hasn't said a word."

His dog, Frank Robert, a Chinese Shar-Pei whom he simply called Frank, raised his head in anticipation and looked at him eagerly. In among the folds and wrinkles so characteristic of the breed, he saw those intense eyes that always hit his soft spot. Eyes that pleaded and begged, that he found hard to resist and made his authority drain away like spilled water. The dog was his weakness and he did nothing to fight it; spoiling the wrinkly little mutt was his greatest pleasure — a pleasure that had resulted in a few too many pounds.

"Come on, fatty," he said. "Let's go out to the car."

The dog jumped up, shot over to the door, and stood there whining; he couldn't get out soon enough. Sejer's apartment was on the twelfth floor, and they always used the stairs, the dog bounding down the steps in a steady, well-practiced rhythm. They came out onto the square and walked over to the car. The dog collapsed in the back seat of the Volvo with a great sigh, true to habit. A baby, Sejer thought, only sixteen months old. Well, it was, in all likelihood, an accident. Or it could have been the mother, unhappy or psychotic, or beside herself with rage at a difficult child. It had happened before. Or the father, or both of them together. That had also happened before. So, drowned in a pond, he thought. Well, well, we'll see. He turned on his blinker and pulled out onto the main road. Again, he felt a faint dizziness, but to his great relief it quickly faded away. He was in the car, so he had to keep a clear head. And always, when the dizziness subsided, he felt hugely optimistic about the future. If it happened when he was driving, he pulled over and stopped right away. But it had passed quickly this time. As though it was just a false alarm and nothing to worry about at all. Dear God, please let it be nothing.

. . .

4

"For goodness' sake, go and see a doctor," his daughter Ingrid had said many a time, but she was particularly vehement the day she saw it for herself. He had suddenly lost his balance and collapsed by the kitchen table. Sejer had retorted that there was probably nothing he could do. It was just something he had to live with. Maybe the arteries at the back of his neck were calcified. The blood wasn't getting to his brain, which is apparently quite common in elderly people. And whether he liked it or not, he's getting older. From here on in, it's a gradual decline.

"Dad," she said, slightly exasperated. "Come on, you're only fifty-five! Go and talk to Erik then, if you don't want to go to your physician."

"But Erik is an ER doctor," he protested. "He won't know about dizziness."

"OK, if you want to be difficult, I can't be bothered talking about it anymore," she said, laughing as always. And every time he heard her laugh, it warmed his heart. But now he had to focus on the dead child found in the pond they call Damtjern. Don't jump to any conclusions, he thought. Be open and clear and considerate. It's important that everything is right, that it's fair. That is what had driven him ever since he was a boy in Gamle Møllevej, and still did in his work as a police inspector in Søndre Buskerud Police District.

A strong and burning desire for truth and justice.

Three vehicles had arrived before he did: Skarre, the forensics team, and an ambulance. They were all leaning against their cars, as there was nothing more they could do. The little boy who had drowned in Damtjern was lying on a tarpaulin. Sejer looked down at the boy. A naked, smooth little body with visible veins. Don't get dizzy now, he thought, not at any cost. Not with people watching.

5

The boy appeared to be well looked after and in good shape with no deformities as far as he could see. His veins were very visible at the temples, a fine web of greenish-blue. His eyes were colorless and dull, but he could tell that they had once been blue; yes, the child was definitely in good shape. If he had suffered any kind of maltreatment, it was certainly not visible.

"The mother said that she went into shock," Skarre told him. "She was doing something in the bathroom, and when she came back into the kitchen he was gone. She ran out into the yard and down to the pond, fearing the worst. She saw him by the jetty, threw herself into the water, and pulled him out. The water was about three feet deep where he was. And she tried to resuscitate him, but couldn't. Well, that's her preliminary statement anyway. We'll see if it changes."

"No visible trauma," Sejer pointed out. "No cuts or bruises. He looks fit and healthy."

He checked his watch; it was half-past two. Wednesday, August 10, beautiful weather, no wind and quite warm. It had been a long, hot summer with almost no rain and the grass around the pond was yellow and dry as straw. And now this—this little body with tiny hands and round cheeks, pale, bluish, and cool as smooth marble.

"Will you call Snorrason?"

"Yes," Sejer replied. "We'll drive the boy's body straight there. We'll get some answers pretty quickly. If he was alive when he fell in the pond, there will be water in his lungs. We might as well start there."

"A sad sight," Skarre said and nodded at the little body.

"Yes," Sejer agreed. "A very sad sight indeed." And I'm dizzy again, he thought to himself, and took a deep breath. He was squatting down next to the dead child and dreaded trying to stand up in case he gave himself away. Then they would find out that he, an inspector, was no longer at his best, but in serious decline. That age had caught up with him, or worse. So he stayed where he was and waited for it to pass.

"Do they live in the white house?" he asked and pointed to the old building with red window-frames.

"Yes," Skarre replied. "And they're very young. Only nineteen and twenty, in fact, so they started early. But, well, he looks a bit odd, doesn't he?"

Sejer studied the small face with colorless cheeks. Yes, there was something special about him, something familiar.

"Down syndrome," he said decisively. "I'd put a bet on it. Look at his eyes; that's where you usually see it. And his hands, at that line, the one that runs across." He lifted the boy's hand to show him. The hand was cold and smooth.

"But he's definitely old enough to walk," he added. "He may even have crawled from the house down to the jetty."

Skarre wandered around in the dry grass. His body was trim and agile, ready for action. His shirt was clean and freshly ironed as always, his shoes shiny. And if these virtues were not enough, he also believed in God. Jacob Skarre had given himself up to the mystery they call faith.

"I wonder why he's naked," Sejer mused. "There must be a reason. But then again, it is warm. Babies only sweat from their heads. Maybe they undressed him because it was so warm."

"It's obviously quite possible that he went down to the pond on his own," Skarre agreed. "It's not far. And most children learn to walk around one. Speaking of which, I didn't start walking until I was eighteen months. My parents couldn't sleep at night, because they thought I was disabled."

"Who'd have guessed it?" Sejer exclaimed. "You who are so nimble?" Then he turned to the forensics team: "Can you drive the body down to Snorrason and say I'm waiting?"

He took a few steps across the grass and stared up at the white house with the dark windows. A swing set added a splash of red and he noticed a small sandbox with some brightly colored toys in it. Three old bikes stood leaning against the wall. A flower bed that needed weeding ran along the front of the house. And a blue Golf was parked by the swing.

"If they're only nineteen and twenty," he said, "I presume they don't have any more children."

"That's right," Skarre confirmed. "Just the one. It doesn't bear thinking about."

Afterward, when the body had been driven away, he went back to the car and let out the dog, who bounded around happily in the grass. Skarre watched the fat little beast with a mildly reprimanding smile.

"No one can accuse you of choosing him for his looks," he commented. "He looks like a dishcloth."

"Beauty is transient," Sejer parried. "I'm sure you know that."

He walked across the small jetty and stood looking out over the water, which was like a mirror. The surface gave away nothing about what had happened.

"Why did you call?" he asked, turning to Skarre. "Tell me your thoughts, and why you brought a couple of forensics with you to what was probably nothing more than a tragic accident."

"I don't know," Skarre said. "The mother seems so artificial. It's difficult to make eye contact and she's very evasive. And, well, alarm bells started to ring, so I didn't want to take any chances. If it is murder, she could get away with it pretty easily," he added. "I don't understand the law on that point, I have to say; a life is a life and we're all of equal value."

"Hmm," he paused. "Not sure everyone would agree with you there. But there's no doubt that the bond between mother and child is special. And her young age might also contribute to a

8

more lenient sentence. Nineteen. Goodness, she started early. It will be easy for the defense to find mitigating circumstances. If there is a case and if we decide to prosecute. But we shouldn't speculate so early on in the process. What's your impression of the boy's father?"

"He is extremely quiet and reserved," Skarre said. "He's barely said a word. They're being held separately. They haven't spoken since they were taken to the station. The mother went back to the house to put on some dry clothes. Holthemann has been looking after them, and he contacted a psychologist from Unicare as it's obviously a crisis situation, whatever happened. Guilty or not, we still have a dead toddler."

Sejer searched for a packet of Fisherman's Friends in his pocket and popped one in his mouth.

"And you?" Skarre asked, looking at him intently. "Have you had any more of those dizzy spells that were bothering you?"

"No," Sejer snapped. "No, I haven't noticed anything. It must have been a virus, passed pretty quickly. Happens, I guess."

"You're an incredibly bad liar," Skarre said, smiling. "Come on, let's measure the distance from the pond to the house. I reckon it's about one hundred and sixty-five feet. And that's nothing for a little lad out exploring."

2

HER BODY WOULD not be still and her hands scuttled around on the table looking for something to do.

"What are you thinking?" she asked, her voice fraught with anxiety. Hmm, Holthemann thought, she's squeaking like a mouse in a cat's paw.

"We don't think anything at the moment," he replied. "Like I said, we have certain procedures. We just need to take down a statement and then you can go. Don't upset yourself about it; it's something we do whenever there's a sudden death. There are rules that have to be followed, so relax."

"He'd just learned to walk," she said. "He was playing on his blanket on the floor, then all of a sudden he wasn't there."

"What were you doing?" Holthemann inquired.

"I was doing the housework. I don't remember exactly; everything's so muddled."

She paused and a deep furrow ran across her forehead.

"I think I was preparing food," she added, having seemingly made up her mind.

"You were making supper?" Holthemann asked in a friendly voice.

She thought again, trying to imagine the situation. Her voice was high and childlike, and Holthemann smiled. The smile made his otherwise stern face a little softer.

"Yes, that's right. I was cleaning a fish. At least, I think I was. And I'm not very good at it, so it took awhile. Yes, sorry, my head is a bit of a mess, but I remember I was preparing the fish. And Nicolai was down in the cellar repairing a bike, because that's his hobby. I just don't understand it," she wailed. "I don't understand!" She burst into tears again, and kneaded the tissue in her hand, unable to control herself. She looked terrified, as if she still could not grasp what had happened, had not fully accepted it—that her child was dead and gone forever. The boy she had loved, because she really had, was now no more than a tiny bundle wrapped in a sheet, on its way to the criminal pathology lab to be examined externally and internally.

"Is there anything I can get you?" the chief superintendent asked. Despite his tough image, he thought it was important to show understanding. "Would you like a drink? Can I get you some water?"

"I just want Nicolai," she sobbed.

The chief leaned forward and patted her on the arm. "You'll be able to speak to a psychologist soon," he said. "He'll help you sort things out in your mind. Because it's all over the place right now, isn't it?"

She started to dry her tears. She was only nineteen years old and she seemed even younger, slender as a reed, with fair, almost white hair. She wore long, dangly earrings and pink nail polish. Her top was far too short and showed her belly, golden-brown after all the sun this summer and adorned with a small, silken pearl in her navel.

"Tommy's only sixteen months old," she cried. "I tried mouth-to-mouth, really I did, but it was too late. His lips were all blue.

I don't know if I did it right either; it looks so easy on TV. And I couldn't do the heart massage, because I didn't dare press too hard. I was scared I'd break his bones, because he's only little. And if I'd broken some of his ribs, they could have punctured his lungs. I kept thinking things like that, because I've heard those things happen."

"Take it easy now," Holthemann said. "We're going to go through everything in detail. The inspector will take statements from you and Nicolai. Then we can draw up the whole incident and make sure we've got it right."

She put her hands on the table and scrunched the tissue into a damp ball.

"But I've said everything I've got to say," she sobbed. "There's nothing more to tell. I found him by the jetty."

She suddenly looked him straight in the eye and was very determined. "I know that it was my fault. You might as well just say it, I know what you're thinking. I should have paid more attention, but I was only away for a few minutes. I only went into the bathroom."

"We'll come back to things like blame later," Holthemann said. "We'll have to establish first if anyone is to blame at all. Sadly, accidents happen every day, and this time it was your turn."

She pushed her chair out from the table, leaned forward over her knees, and stayed like that for some time, as if she was about to faint.

"There're spots dancing in front of my eyes," she said, exhausted. Her voice was thin and frail, barely audible.

"Yes, it's the stress," Holthemann explained. "It affects the muscles around your eyes, but it's not dangerous. Just relax. Try to breathe normally and it will pass."

"I just want to talk to Nicolai," she begged. "Is he sitting somewhere all on his own?"

"No, he's with an officer. I'll go and get you something to drink. And then we'll contact your parents. They live here in town, don't they?"

"Yes, they live in Møllergata," she said. "Mom won't be able to cope with this, nor will Dad. He's already had one heart attack. The year before last, and we were beside ourselves. I don't see why I have to sit here," she complained. "I want to be with Nicolai; you can't refuse me. Damn you!"

Holthemann didn't have an answer. He often fell a bit short when it came to people in need. But everything had been done on Jacob Skarre's request: he'd said that this was an accidental drowning that they might want to investigate in more detail, just in case. He got up, left her alone in the room, and went to the staff room where there was a fridge full of cold drinks. He took out a bottle of mineral water and walked back before he realized that he'd forgotten to take a plastic cup from the holder. He headed back to the staff room, got one, and returned to the room where she was sitting. He handed her the cup and helped her open the bottle.

"You will get all the support and understanding you're entitled to, believe me. Now, have a drink," he ordered. "The shock is making you thirsty."

3

MAYBE HE'D BEEN killed, thrown in the pond, unwanted by his mother, Sejer thought. Or by his father, or both. A child who was different, a deviant—perhaps in some people's eyes, a loser. A sudden rage, a mean thought, an urge to destroy. Or was he seeing ghosts in broad daylight? The door into the garden was open. There was no one watching the boy and he tottered out of the house and across the dry grass on his plump little legs, walking the short distance from the house to the jetty. Drawn by the glittering water that lay like a mirror in front of him. I'm not being prejudiced, Sejer thought. I must take absolutely every possibility into consideration. I've done this job long enough, that's how I work. Anything is possible in this case. A simple, clear rule that always helped him focus. Too many bitter experiences, he thought, and I don't like to be duped or lied to. As he drove, he thought about his parents again, and all that they had given him as a little boy. Love and understanding, leniency. Encouragement and confidence, an understanding that life was not easy, for better or for worse. Careful now, he said to himself; they're probably both innocent. But Skarre had expressed clear concern. He thought about it and what it might mean. Intuition was important and definitely had a role to play in every investigation. Having a feeling about something, the seed of suspicion that something is wrong. It might be a lack of eye contact or a strange distance to what had happened. A body that won't be still, restless and nervous hands, a monotone voice when giving a statement. The sequence of events rattled off as if learned by rote, a kind of planned version. A hand that constantly dabs the eyes to dry imaginary tears or, for that matter, real tears. Because everything had gone so terribly wrong, with or without blame. Or horror that an emotion could be so catastrophic. I'm going to kill you now because it's unbearable. I can't stand this child, can't cope with this child, and other impossible emotions. All these different signs of lies. And a depressing thought kept coming back. The child had Down syndrome. Another reason for this unease. Even though the public prosecutor would only consider the facts of the case, these gut instincts were incredibly important. They were based on the experience that they had built up over all their years with the police. Skarre had noticed some nuances that he couldn't explain, that had made him think twice. Sejer took this seriously because Skarre was smart. And pretty good in his observations. Two parents sitting in the station crying their hearts out, but were they tears of loss and grief, or were they tears of shock and panic because they were guilty?

He started to think about the recurring dizzy spells again. I'll have to bite the bullet, he thought, and haul my decrepit body off to the doctor. It's all downhill from here. Then I'll have to endure a whole raft of tests and the nerve-racking wait. Maybe there really is something terribly wrong with me, and life as I've known it until now is—well, maybe it's over. The word *cancer* popped up in his thoughts again, thoughts that would not let him be. He suddenly felt the need for moral support and dialed the number of his daughter Ingrid, to tell her about the incident at Damtjern.

"Hi, Ingrid, it's me. Yes, I'm in the car. Yes, yes, I'm using the hands-free; don't be silly. We've found a little boy. He was lying in a pond up by Granfoss. His mother found him by the jetty. Just over a year. It's so sad. Yes, exactly, I'm on my way to the station. I'm going to talk to the parents. Maybe I'll drop by afterward, if that's all right?"

"Yes," she said. "Of course that's all right. And how are you otherwise, Dad?"

She meant the dizziness. He said he was sure it would pass and it was just a matter of patience. But she wasn't going to let him get away with such a vague answer.

"It'll pass? Don't give me happily ever after; I'm too old for that. I know you," she continued, "you're not telling me everything. But you don't need to spare me; remember that I've been through a lot. And just so you know, I can stomach the truth."

She was referring to her stint as a nurse in war-torn Somalia with her husband, Erik, who specialized in acute medicine. When they came back home, after working there for several years, they had a boy with them. Sejer's only grandchild was now a promising young dancer with the National Ballet School.

"OK," he said. "I promise, I won't spare you. And yes, I am still dizzy. I mean, every now and then. But I promise I'm going to do something about it, once and for all." He was at the railroad crossing in the center of town, and the barrier was down. While he sat and waited for the train to pass, he thought about the little boy again. What Skarre had said was right. If this was actually murder, and it was the mother who had done it, she would get off lightly. That special bond between mother and child, so many mitigating circumstances, so many possible explanations. *Non compos mentis,* he thought, not of sound mind. Personality disorders, psychosis, depression, and other complaints. There was so much to choose from. A freight train with dark red cars finally thundered past. He listened to the steady rhythm of the wheels and the rattling of iron and metal, and he counted the cars, as he had done since childhood.

He could not help but think of a dandelion head with its delicate white pappi, because her hair was almost as white as snow. He was also struck by how slight she was, thin and fragile as a twig. A child with a child, he thought. It was incredible that she had managed to give birth to a baby at all.

"Come with me," he said in a reassuring voice. "Let's go to my office; it's just a bit farther down the corridor."

She got to her feet and then saw the dog. Frank stood up on his hind legs, wanting to say hello. She stroked him gingerly on the head, but she seemed to be elsewhere. The catastrophe had drained her of color and she had dark rings under her eyes.

"If he bothers you, I'll put him in the car," Sejer said. "But usually he settles down; he doesn't normally make a fuss."

She shook her head. But she did keep looking at the dog, as if he touched something in her, some longing.

"What is your name?" he asked as kindly as he could, as they walked down the corridor.

"Carmen," she replied. "Carmen Cesilie Zita."

Her name sounded familiar. And before he could ask, she had given him the answer.

"Yes," she said, as though reading his thoughts. "My father owns the fast-food place in Torggata. The one called Zita Quick. He's had it for ten years, and we both work there. Well, I don't really at the moment because Tommy's still so little. But Nicolai does shifts there. We're open all night."

She paused and looked at Sejer with blue eyes surrounded by thick black lashes. "People come all the way from Oslo for our food," she said proudly.

He opened the door to his office. Frank slipped in, went over to the blanket by the window, and lay down.

"Please, find yourself a chair," he told her.

He studied the slight girl.

"My condolences, Carmen," he added. "It's terribly sad."

He wanted to be friendly. Wanted to do everything right, in case she wasn't guilty.

"Why can't I be with Nicolai?" she asked. But the question was also a complaint and she sounded petulant. You don't just plow your way into someone else's life; you tiptoe in with care and respect. So he weighed his words carefully. He had considerable training.

"You have to be separated, as a matter of procedure," he explained patiently. "I can understand if you might find it a bit brutal, but we automatically follow lots of rules and regulations, so there is absolutely no need to worry about it. We're going to talk together for a while, and then afterward you can both go home to Granfoss. Oh, I see you didn't take your mineral water with you. Shall I get you another one?"

She shook her head and sat down in a chair by the window. She wasn't interested in the view; her eyes were fixed on her hands, which she had folded in her lap. But she glanced over at Frank every now and then. The dog lying on the gray blanket was obviously soothing.

"What was your little boy's name?" he asked. "Tommy?"

He rolled his chair across the floor and sat down beside her.

"Yes, his name is Tommy Nicolai."

She started to cry. And while she cried, he sat and waited patiently until the outburst was over.

"Now, let's go through it all again," he said. "Step by step. Exactly as it happened. You can tell me your own way, if you like. Or if you think that's difficult, I can ask you questions."

"Maybe you should ask questions," she said. "Everything's just chaos; it's so hard to remember."

"I understand," Sejer assured her. "I'll ask you questions then. Now tell me about the day. What were you doing when you discovered that Tommy had disappeared?"

He could see that she was rifling through her memory; her eyes darted around the room, returning to Frank again, who had fallen asleep on his blanket.

"Well, it was getting on for supper time. I'd decided we were going to have salmon. So that's probably what I was doing, preparing the fish."

"Probably? You're not sure?"

"Yes, of course I'm sure. Don't talk to me like I'm some stupid little girl."

But she paused and didn't seem certain at all. Sejer reminded himself that she was most likely in shock, so her memory would have gaps; he'd seen it before. Likewise, angry words would spill over in the heat of the moment.

"Do you feel uncertain, Carmen?" he asked again.

"The whole day is just a blur," she said curtly. She wrung her hands. She was on guard; he knew the signs.

"And Tommy's dad? What did you say his name was?"

"Nicolai Brandt. And we're married. I know what you're thinking, that we're young and silly, and we lack judgment."

"Not at all," he said. "I would never think that. Where was Nicolai when it happened? Tell me."

"He was down in the cellar repairing some old bikes. He earns a bit of money doing simple repairs and gets quite a few jobs. He loves messing around with bikes; he's obsessed. So he wasn't there

19

when it happened. I was alone in the kitchen and Tommy was sitting on a blanket on the floor. He had no clothes on because it was so hot and I wanted him to get some air. He often gets very sweaty. I'd opened the back door to get a draft through."

Sejer noted her body language and the pitch of her voice. She was now very focused and calm, as though she finally felt in control of the difficult situation. But her voice was monotonous, and he knew that this detail could signal distance. That she was keeping something terrible at a distance, which she simply couldn't face.

"Then I had to go to the bathroom," she continued. "A chore I had to do in there. It took awhile. And when I came back, he'd gone. He wasn't sitting on his blanket, and the room was empty. Tommy has just learned to walk," she explained, "and he's pretty good. He can get quite far in a minute, and I'd been away for a while. First I ran into the bedroom. I even checked under the comforter, because, you see, I panicked right away. Then I ran out of the house and looked around. But I couldn't see him any-where—not in the sandbox, not behind the house. I couldn't even bear to think about the pond. Even though it was a constant threat, I pushed it out of my mind. But I went down in the end, because I had to look everywhere. And then I saw him by the jetty. He was lying face down under the water. I threw myself into the water without even thinking. I managed to get him out onto the grass. And I shouted as loud as I could for Nicolai. Eventually he came running out in a panic. It was so strange, because I heard the screams, but I didn't recognize my own voice. Do you know what I mean?"

She stopped talking and put her hand up to wipe away a stray tear.

"But we couldn't revive him. He was gone. Nicolai called an ambulance and they came really fast, and they tried to revive him as well. They tried and tried for ages, maybe as long as an hour; you should have seen the effort they made. But it didn't help. No matter what they did, Tommy was gone."

Sejer sat and listened to the monotone explanation. He was observing her the entire time: her voice, her facial expression, and other signs. She could absolutely be telling the truth. Things like that had happened so many times before, younger and older children falling in the water, mostly when they were playing. But there was also a chance that she was putting it on, acting. She had a theatrical manner that was slightly artificial. And she was certainly very affected, concerned about her appearance and what people thought of her, because her back was straight and her chin tilted up.

"Was Tommy a healthy boy?" he asked.

"Oh yes," she said with some force. "Yes. He has Down syndrome, but apart from that he's very healthy. He's never been sick or anything like that. Well, actually, he did once get an ear infection. And his temperature rocketed, so we had to take him to the ER in the middle of the night. But then he was given some medicine and he got well right away. Well, after a couple of days, that is. But apart from that, nothing."

"How did the fact that he had Down syndrome affect your daily life? Can you say a bit about that?"

"Well, you know, he needed a bit more help. They develop very slowly and they don't learn as fast as other children," she explained. "But I'm sure you knew that."

"How was it to live in a house by Damtjern with a baby?" Sejer asked. "Were you constantly worried about the pond?"

She nodded and said that it was dangerous with such a young child to have a deep and alluring pond so close to the house.

"But we couldn't go around being scared all the time," she said. "After all, plenty of people live by the water. Children grow up by the sea. Two children in two years have drowned down by Stranda. I know things like that happen. And now it's happened to us."

"Yes," he said and nodded. "What you're saying is true, of course. But I'd like to ask you another question. You're very young to be a mother. Was Tommy a wanted child? I mean, was he planned?"

"Yes, we wanted him," she said. "I mean, I didn't use anything, and neither did Nicolai. So we weren't exactly surprised to find out I was pregnant. And I was so happy when I saw the test was positive. We were over the moon. We whooped and danced around the kitchen like kids. So, there's your answer," she added, with a wan smile. "Of course he was wanted. Wanted with all my heart, you have to believe me."

"And then," Sejer continued thoughtfully, "Tommy finally came into the world. Tell me about the pregnancy; what did it feel like to be pregnant? You've got such a slim figure and a baby is quite a weight to carry."

"Oh no," she livened up and spoke with enthusiasm. "Everything was great. It was an easy pregnancy, and I felt wonderful. Everyone said I looked great too. And I felt absolutely fine the whole time. I didn't put on much weight either and Tommy only weighed six pounds. Nicolai teased us all the time. Said that Tommy looked like a little buttermilk pudding, all white and smooth."

"What sort of baby was he?" Sejer asked. "Was he a happy baby?"

"Yes," she said and nodded. "A very happy baby. He occasionally had trouble sleeping, but we coped. We took turns getting up at night. And sometimes we argued, but generally we coped well."

"Did you breastfeed him?"

"No, no, I didn't."

"Why not? Did you not have milk?"

"I didn't want to breastfeed," she said sullenly. "You can see what I look like; I wasn't made for that sort of thing." She was referring to her flat chest, where two slight mounds were in evidence under the cropped, tight top.

He noticed a sudden fleeting reluctance, as if he had touched a sore point that she didn't want to talk about. She clammed up and became unreachable. And he thought, as he looked at the small girl sitting beside him in her ripped jeans, that she was perhaps to blame for her son's death. That she had done something improper, that she was guilty of a crime. Maybe the very worst kind. He thought like this out of habit; to be fair, it was a hazard of the job. Suspicion. To doubt people. Take nothing for granted. And at the same time he tried not to be judgmental. Then he wondered how, if this really was a murder case, they would ever manage to prove it when there were no witnesses? When the mother claimed that the toddler had gone down to the water on his own when no one was watching him. While she was in the bathroom. And a big filleted fish was lying on the counter.

"He was an adventurous little boy," Carmen said. "He wanted to explore and look at everything. Inside the house he crawled around at the speed of light. It was hard to keep up with him," she said, drying a tear. "I was always so worried that he might hurt himself."

She was over the first hurdle now and could see things from a different angle, what had happened down by the water, the great tragedy. The words flowed easily and she said that she was not to blame and that it was an accident. Sejer made a mental note that she had distanced herself from the tragedy. She was able to keep it at arm's length, for the moment at least. But it wouldn't last long, he thought; reality would soon come crashing over her like a wave. What had happened, in all its horror, would stay with her. Every day for the rest of her life. And on the day that she herself lay dying, the day when she no longer had a future, she would think back and remember it in detail. The child face down in the black water.

"How long have you and Nicolai been living together?" he asked in a calm voice.

"Two years," she replied. "But we've been together for four. I was only fifteen when we met. I had a boyfriend before him, but it only lasted for a month, because I couldn't trust him. So it's always been us. We work well together. Even though we're very different, there's no denying it."

"Different in what way?"

"Nicolai is slow and methodical," she said, "whereas I'm fast and impulsive, if you see what I mean."

"Was he a good father?"

"Oh yes, the best. Much more patient than me. He never gets desperate or angry and he's always kind. He's not particularly quick. He's more the careful kind, but he's totally dependable."

"And did he try to give first aid as well?"

"Yes, we both did. But we could see it was too late; we could see that he was blue. It was horrible. And Nicolai had to call for the ambulance because I was completely hysterical and couldn't do anything. Can we refuse to have an autopsy?" she asked abruptly. "Sorry for asking, but it's just such a horrible thought, because I know what they do, I've read about it in the papers. And I don't want anyone poking around in Tommy's body."

Sejer noted her use of the phrase "poking around" and her aversion to closer examinations, but did not draw any conclusions. He had come across the problem before, often in relation to suicides or crib deaths. People wanted to bury their loved ones whole, which was perfectly understandable.

"But the autopsy will be very important," he said. "It might give us lots of answers."

"But I found him in the water," she countered. "He drowned. The cause of death is obvious, so I don't see the point."

"Carmen," Sejer said patiently, "this is what we call a sudden and unexpected death. And it is routine to do an autopsy. Take my word for it, he will be treated with the utmost care."

This made her less willing to talk. She clammed up again and avoided catching his eye as she sat there twiddling a silver ring with a red stone around her finger. Maybe she was tired, or maybe she was nervous; it was hard to tell. Sejer, who was now more prone to suspect, started to push her a bit. There were no doubt far too many child murders that had never been proven and so wrongly filed as accidents. Children, as the most vulnerable in society, have a right to justice, he thought, once again touching on his childhood ideals. Everything that his father had taught him: law, truth, and justice.

"Can I call my dad?" she asked. "I have to call him and explain. They've only got me," she added. "And Tommy is their only grandchild."

Then she started crying again, bitter tears.

"I did have a sister, but she's dead," she explained. "And this will be too much for them. Dad's got a bad heart and Mom's just really nervous."

"Carmen," Sejer said in a calm voice, "you do have rights, and I'm not going to deny you any of them. But you must prepare yourself for some very difficult conversations. That's just the way it is, but it is all done with the best intentions. Don't be afraid; I'm sure we'll manage to work this out together."

She glanced over at Frank, who was still asleep on his blanket. And then she looked straight at Sejer again. Her eyes were fraught with doubt.

"Am I suspected of something?"

Sejer let her stew in uncertainty for a while. He had the same feeling as Skarre, that something was amiss. Her behavior was odd, given the tragedy, and this made him push her more.

"As I said, we need to find out exactly what happened," he told her. "An officer will examine your house, but, again, it is simply a matter of routine. So you don't need to worry."

Carmen stared at him. "What? The house? He died in the pond. I don't understand!" She burst into tears again and brushed a lock of hair from her face. "There's nothing to see in the house," she continued. "I don't understand how you're even allowed to do that. Examine the house! To look for what?"

Sejer got up from the chair, moving it so they were sitting face to face. Being confronted in this way made her even more uncertain and upset.

"Well, I mean, I don't want to make a fuss," she said. "I just think it's all so weird. It's hard to take in. Is it you who's going to talk to Nicolai?"

"Yes, I will talk to Nicolai. To hear his version and see if it corresponds with yours. You do understand that's how we have to work, don't you?"

"But it does correspond," she said hastily, about to start crying again. "You don't think I'm sitting here lying, do you?"

4

ON THE PORCH, some jackets and coats on a row of hooks. Two pairs of hiking boots, a pair of rain boots, some shoes on a shoe rack. A knotted plastic bag, presumably with garbage in it to be taken down to the garbage can along the road. A door down to the cellar with its mysterious murkiness. Inside, a dresser and mirror in the hallway, a lonely jacket with reflective stripes on the arms. To the right, a small living room with a sofa and coffee table. The room was dominated by a flat-screen TV, maybe fifty inches wide. Two armchairs, one with a footstool. Lots of books on the bookshelves, including some large ones about animals and birds. Next to the living room, a dining room with a table and four chairs, and a desk with a Mac desktop on it.

Skarre went from room to room, paying attention to all the details. Shriveled potted plants, magazines on the table. A remote control and an empty Coke can, a blanket with red fringe on the sofa. A play blanket on the floor with pockets and bells. On the wall, a black-and-white photograph of a child, taken by a good amateur photographer—perhaps Nicolai. The Down syndrome was obvious in his eyes and his short, stocky body and square hands. He was standing in a field full of daisies and dandelions, wearing nothing but a diaper. It had indeed been a hot summer. Every man and his dog had shed all the clothes they could. He stood looking at the photograph for a long time and was filled with sorrow as he stared at the little boy. He eventually pulled himself together and moved on to the bedroom. He paused in the doorway and felt that he was entering somewhere private. He always felt like this, like a voyeur, stomping around in someone else's life, but he had to do it. So he shook off the feeling, went into the room, and walked over to the window. The pond could not be seen from this side of the house, and he looked out onto a cluster of trees. There were no other houses nearby. Two single beds had been pushed together to make a double. One of the bedside tables was tidy and neat, the other full of stuff: an alarm clock, nasal spray, tissues, a glass of water. A watch, a hairbrush, and a bottle of acetaminophen in case of a temperature or headache. The bed linen was blue with white clouds, no doubt from Ikea. An old worn teddy bear lay on the bed, staring blindly at him with black glass eyes. And in the corner was the boy's white crib with a mobile above it, four flying birds with red feathers. There was also a teddy bear here, but it was new and looked expensive. Maybe a present from his grandparents. Whereas the old worn one had been abandoned, relegated to the grown-up bed. From there, into the bathroom. Some socks hanging up to dry. Otherwise little of interest. He went back into the living room, sat down on the sofa, and dialed Sejer's number.

"Nothing of any note," he said. "No great discoveries. Just normal, everyday mess."

"Where are you now?"

"In the living room."

"Well, go into the kitchen," Sejer instructed, "and I expect you'll find a fish there. Is there anything else on the counter, the makings of supper?"

Skarre went and looked around the tidy kitchen.

"Yep, looks like salmon, and it's partially cleaned. Happy now?

Otherwise nothing. Socks drying in the bathroom, some mess by the bed, just day-to-day things. An empty whiskey bottle on the counter so one of them drinks, presumably Nicolai."

"What makes you say that?"

"Girls that age don't drink whiskey," Skarre said.

"No, you're probably right," Sejer agreed. "So far Carmen is telling the truth then. But I have to admit, she does seem a bit confused regarding the sequence of events. Call me if you find anything else. In the meantime, I'll speak to Nicolai, and we'll see if they say the same thing."

"So what are your thoughts?" Skarre asked.

"Well, the usual, I suppose, that one of them might be lying. And if that's the case, then the guilty party is not going to get away with it."

5

"IT WAS TOO late," Nicolai Brandt said. "He was all blue. That is, his nails and lips were blue, and otherwise he was white as a sheet. I could see that it was Tommy, but he looked so alien. I realized that he was dead, and Carmen was completely hysterical. It was impossible to think. It was all wrong, what I did. I'm useless," he said melodramatically as he dried a tear.

"Where were you when she shouted for help?" Sejer asked.

"In the cellar," Nicolai replied. "I was repairing a bike. I earn a bit of money doing little jobs like that. It was a friend's bike. I had changed and oiled the chain, so it was fixed."

"So," Sejer said patiently, "you were bent over the bicycle. What did you think when you heard Carmen shout?"

"She wasn't shouting; she was screaming," Nicolai said. "I knew right away that Tommy was in the water. I've always hated that pond and worried about it all the time. Tommy's all over the place, because he's just learned to walk, and he couldn't get enough. So I let go of the bike and ran as fast as I could down to the pond. Carmen had managed to get him out of the water and onto the grass. We did everything we could to revive him, but nothing worked. He didn't react. I called for an ambulance and they came as fast as they could, but I realized after only a few minutes that it was already too late. They tried to resuscitate him too, but didn't manage either—even though they were better at it than us and had done it loads of times. We could tell that they were professionals and had probably saved many lives. So I kept hoping. Waiting for him to wake and cough up some water. For him to get the color back in his face and to start breathing again."

Nicolai was extremely pale despite the long summer, and his eyes were dark pools of grief and despair. It was perhaps the first time he had seen death up close. He was only twenty, after all. And everyone's first experience of death is traumatic.

"So," Sejer started after a pause, "had Tommy walked down to the pond before? It's not that far really, only about one hundred and sixty feet. Or had he gone outside onto the grass by himself before or anything like that? Can you remember any episodes?"

Nicolai clenched his hands in his lap. He was also of slight build, like Carmen, so they were well matched, these two unhappy souls. He had thin hair that was slicked back and long at the neck. There was a small tattoo that looked like a Japanese character on one hand.

"What does your tattoo mean?" Sejer asked out of curiosity.

"Courage," Nicolai told him.

"Does it work?"

"No, not at all. I've always been a coward. Could we be charged with negligence?"

Sejer ignored the question.

"Why do you say that you're a coward?" he asked. "Who says you're a coward?"

"I do. I know I am; you don't need to humor me. Because I don't deserve it."

"All right then," Sejer said, wanting to move on. "Tommy. Had he ever gone out of the house on his own before? Out into the garden?"

"Yes, a couple of times. When he got to the steps, he'd crawl.

I've told Carmen to keep all the doors shut, because he's so quick. But it was a warm day and the doors were wide open."

"Can you tell me what Carmen was doing when Tommy disappeared? Do you know?"

He thought about it, running his tattooed hand through his hair.

"I don't know. She was doing the housework, I guess. Or making supper. She enjoys it, just puttering around doing things. She likes making food; she's very domestic."

"And where do you work, Nicolai?"

"I work with Pappa Zita in the center of town. At Zita Quick, the fast-food place on Torggata."

"And do you like working for your father-in-law?"

"Yes, he's really nice. But he had a major heart attack a couple of years ago, so he has to take things easy now. Carmen and I help him as much as we can. We don't earn very much, but we get by on what we've got. Carmen's still on maternity leave, but she'll start working again, once Tommy —"

He stopped abruptly, remembering everything. Frank got up from where he had been sleeping and went over to him. He stood licking Nicolai's hand with his warm tongue.

"Do you like dogs?" Sejer asked to distract him.

He nodded and stroked Frank's wrinkly head. "Yes, Carmen does too. But we didn't get one because of Tommy. I mean, we'd thought of waiting until he was three or four. I realize now it's stupid to put things off. Suddenly life is over," he said, "and it's too late. The house will be so empty now. We're used to hearing him laugh and cry; I don't know how we'll manage!" He burst into tears. Sitting helplessly in his chair, he tried to dry his eyes.

"You'll be offered support from a psychologist," Sejer assured him. "Do you think you'll take it?"

"No, I don't believe in talking. I just want to be left alone," he said. "Will we be able to go home soon? I don't understand all these questions, and they're upsetting me."

"Yes, you'll be able to go home soon. We'll contact you again once we've got the results from the autopsy."

Nicolai shook his head despondently. "But there's nothing to find," he said. "Can we not be spared that?"

"I'm sorry," Sejer said firmly, "but the circumstances make it necessary. And even if you don't understand why we need to do an autopsy, I can assure you that it's in Tommy's interests. We have procedures that need to be followed; can you trust me on this one?"

"I just think it's so awful," he mumbled. "I can't bear the thought of it, opening up his little body and emptying out the contents."

"You won't be able to tell afterward, I promise you that," Sejer said. "Rest assured that you will be able to see him for a last time without being upset. Talk to the funeral directors about it. They can help you with things like that."

Nicolai sat in silence for a long time, lifting his gaze to look out of the window, while Sejer thought about Carmen. What would her motive have been, if she had in fact thrown Tommy in the pond on purpose? That she couldn't take any more? That he wasn't a wanted child, as she claimed he was? That he tied her down? That having a child who was different felt like a burden—an overwhelming, lifelong, all-encompassing, and exhausting obligation that was simply too much? And so today, of all days, on Wednesday, August 10, she had done what she could to get rid of him once and for all? Simply because he was different. Could that really be true? Or was it none of the above. Just a tragic accident of the kind they saw too many of, where no one was to blame?

It was six o'clock in the evening when he let them go. Skarre drove them back to the house. He stood outside and looked around. It was a long way to the nearest neighbors; there were no houses in the immediate vicinity. Something criminal could easily have happened down at the pond that day without another living soul seeing anything.

tions. Your leg"—he changed the subject and nodded at Holthe-mann's leg—"is it still alive?"

"Only just," Holthemann replied gloomily. "I've got practically no feeling in it; it's just numb."

"Get yourself on a treadmill," Sejer suggested. "It'll improve your circulation."

The chief shook his head. "No," he said firmly. "What will be, will be. No one is going to get me to run like a rat in a wheel."

7

Evening.

Carmen watched him from the window. She stood there for a while, wringing her hands. Nicolai had walked across the yard and onto the jetty. Now he was sitting on the edge and looked terrible. She went down after him, slowly, hesitantly, uncertain what to say. The words she was so frantically trying to catch seemed to grow like toads in her mouth, and suddenly she felt thirsty.

"Nicolai," she said gently, "he's never coming back. And we have to deal with it somehow. The future, I mean, and how we cope. Come inside, Nicolai. We have to eat; it's getting late." She stood on the jetty and begged and pleaded. But Nicolai was ashen with grief, his thin brown hair bedraggled. She had never seen him like this before, never seen him so helpless and forsaken.

"How can you think about food," he said, "when Tommy's gone forever? I just don't get how you can think about food."

She sat down beside him and took him by the arm. Her nails against his skin felt like sharp claws.

"If we don't eat, then we'll die too. And Tommy wouldn't have wanted that," she said seriously.

Nicolai flared up, unable to help himself.

"You know nothing about what Tommy would want," he said, his voice bitter. "You should have shut the door. You know what he's like, that he gets everywhere. People say those children are slow, but not our Tommy. He was quick as lightning."

"Yes, but it was so hot," she complained. "And you were in the cellar as usual. It's nice and cool down there, so it's easy for you to talk. You don't need to put the blame on me," she added.

"That's not fair. It's bad enough as it is, without you making it worse. We're going to have to talk sometime. We have to sort out the funeral and a whole lot of other things. Pappa Zita will be here soon; he'll help us get started."

Nicolai picked at a loose splinter in the dark wood with nails that were bitten to the quick.

"What did they ask you about?" she said after a pause. "They asked me all kinds of things. They even wanted to know if I breastfed him. I don't see why they have to go into such detail. It just seems nosy to me."

"You don't understand anything, do you? You don't get how serious this is. Tommy's dead and gone. He drowned, and it's our fault because we didn't keep an eye on him. He wanted to know what you were doing when Tommy left the house. What were you doing?"

She thought about it. "I was just puttering around, tidying up, you know. And I wanted to clean the fish for supper. I went into the bathroom to rinse out some washing. Everything happened so fast. And I looked for him in all the rooms before I even thought about the pond. Come on now, we have to go in," she nagged. "Mom and Dad will be here soon, and they'll help us with supper."

"You and your supper," he snapped. "Just go and stuff your

face, why don't you. I'm not going anywhere. If your dad wants anything, he can come down here to the jetty, because this is where I'm going to be all night."

She stood up, exasperated and desperate. She looked out at the water and the single water lily. Strange that there was only one, so beautiful and white and delicate. And then she spoke without thinking, the words falling from her mouth before she had a chance to stop them.

"We can have another one. We're so young."

Nicolai let out a small gasp, as if the thought was monstrous.

"I want to move," he said quickly. "I don't want to live by the water, not with children. And I don't want another one; can you just stop?"

She didn't reply. Instead she started to walk back to the house, and he followed her slender body with his eyes. There was something strange about her behavior, the way she was walking in her cropped top. In spite of everything, her steps were quick and light, as if she was unaffected by it all. Then a terrible thought struck him, and a shiver ran down his spine despite the warmth in the air. The fact that she seemed so indifferent, that she wanted to engage in life again right away, even though they were in mourning. A deep, bottomless pit of grief. He couldn't even contemplate food or sleep or work, or the days ahead that would roll on regardless.

"Are you coming?" she turned around and called.

"Didn't I just say no?" he yelled.

Suddenly he couldn't contain himself any longer.

"Go, just go. Go and get on with your life!"

She stood there looking at him, astounded by this outburst. She didn't recognize him, didn't know this fury. She had never seen it before.

"Do you want a divorce?" she asked out of the blue. Now she was angry as well, because he was being so horrible and difficult.

"Yes," he said. "Maybe I do. Then you can grieve in your own weird way."

8

MORE THAN ANYTHING, he wanted to keep her in his shirt pocket, close to his heart. He wanted to take her everywhere with him and protect her from all fear and suffering, protect her from all danger. Because he loved Carmen Cesilie more than anything in the world, this slip of a blond thing who was his daughter. He had a father's unstinting patience. He held her to him tight, bursting with love. She disappeared into his embrace and stayed there for a long time. Marian Zita was big and heavy, with a sturdy barrel-shaped body, thin legs, and broad duck's feet. He had thick, curly black hair peppered with gray, and huge worn hands that were used to hard work. In private, Zita had cursed God and the Virgin, all the deities who had betrayed him, raging with sorrow and despair. Carmen cried against his chest, inconsolable. Her father had always been her loyal ally; he stood by her through thick and thin no matter what. And over the years there had been a number of times when she needed his help. Like the time when the boyfriend she had before Nicolai had hit her. And when she became pregnant with Tommy at seventeen. But this was a crisis. Her mother looked around the yard, then further down toward the water, where she saw Nicolai sitting at the end of the jetty.

"How do you think he feels? Shall we go and comfort him?"

"No," Carmen said. "He doesn't want it. He just wants to be left alone. He says he's going to sit there all night. He's not very good at expressing his emotions—he clams up completely. And then there's nothing you can do. He just says no. Come on; let's go in. Maybe he'll come later. Maybe he'll change his mind."

Her parents followed her into the house. When her mother saw Tommy's play blanket on the floor, she started to cry.

"Why didn't we manage to get the fence sorted?" Zita said wearily. "It will haunt me until my dying day. We could have hired a carpenter; it would have been done in no time."

Carmen pulled out a chair and sat down at the kitchen table.

"We need to eat something," she said, determined. "When I said that to Nicolai, that we needed food, he got mad at me. I mean, making sure we get sustenance is not exactly being disloyal to Tommy, is it?"

She caught her father's eye, seeking the comfort she always got. A right that she had taken for granted all her life.

"Is it, Dad?" she begged. "I'm hungry. I haven't eaten all day. It isn't being disloyal to Tommy if we eat."

Her father shook his head. "No, sweetheart, of course not. And no matter what Nicolai says, I'm going down to see him."

Carmen grabbed his arm. "He says it's my fault," she said. "That I should have closed the door and kept an eye on him."

Her father waved his hands around in exasperation. He almost lost his balance. "What has happened is terrible, but it was an accident," he said. "And no one at all is to blame, especially not you. He just said that in despair. He doesn't know what he's saying and he'll regret it later. I know how it is in the heat of the moment. Don't forget your sister, Louisa," he added with feeling. "I know what I'm talking about."

He stroked her cheek.

"And you know, that's the thing about grief," he continued.

"We're no longer rational and it's hard to think straight. Words just pop out of our mouths that we later live to regret."

He went out, crossed the yard, and lumbered down to the jetty. The dark planks creaked under his considerable weight.

"How are things?" he asked in a friendly voice. "How are you?"

Nicolai shrugged and kept his eyes focused on the only water lily in the pond. He felt Zita's large hand on his neck. It was a strong, patriarchal hand that spoke of authority.

"Not good," he said with a sigh. "I'm not managing this at all. I'm just sitting here, and I don't intend to move."

Zita stood without saying anything for a while. He understood Nicolai's bleak thoughts about the future only too well. Life had not been good to him.

"I don't know what to do," Zita said eventually. "I don't know how to comfort you; there is no comfort. There is nothing I can say."

He tried to catch his son-in-law's eye and sat down beside him with his feet dangling over the edge.

"All it takes is a few moments when you're not paying attention," he continued. "Everything happens so fast. You have my full sympathy. We'll support you in every way, you know that. You can count on us." He raised his voice when he said this and sounded more determined.

"You'll have all the time you need to grieve. No one can deny you the right to give up. To cry and rage and curse fate. But let me just say one thing." Zita took a deep breath and said loudly: "I will not allow you ever to blame my daughter."

Nicolai didn't say anything for a while. He turned away from the water lily and looked at his father-in-law with melancholy eyes.

"There's a lot you don't know," he said.

"And what is that supposed to mean?" Zita asked promptly. "Explain yourself."

"It's not always easy to put a finger on it," Nicolai tried. "Put it that way."

Zita felt uneasy. He didn't like the implication and couldn't understand the cryptic message.

"Don't make things difficult," he said sternly. "Tell me what's on your mind; I don't like these insinuations. Come on; let's go up to the house. We've got a lot to talk about. And forgive me for saying so, but you're not the only one who's grieving. This is a terrible blow for all of us."

Nicolai did not want to talk, as he had little belief in the ability of words to heal and soothe. And yet he stood up, somewhat reluctantly, and walked back toward the house. He stopped on the lawn and looked around with set lips. Everything seemed different and new, not the well-loved, familiar landscape he was used to being a part of. We should have put up a fence, he thought, as he watched Pappa Zita roll up to the house. A fence around the whole house with a latched gate. A simple solution that could have saved Tommy's life, but it was too late now. He followed Zita into the house and let his mother-in-law, Elsa, embrace him. She had always been shy, but she was unable to contain herself and held him as tight as she could while her tears flowed. He pulled himself free and went into the living room. He turned on the TV, sat in a chair, and watched the news without moving. He stared almost blindly at the flickering images. There's always someone who's got it worse, he thought, but that's cold comfort. He got up wearily and went back into the kitchen.

"We have to choose an undertaker," Pappa Zita said. "Not the biggest or most expensive; let's use a smaller one. Sentrum," he suggested, "I hear they're very good, even though there are only two of them. When will we get Tommy back from the coroner?"

Carmen and Nicolai looked at each other. Neither of them could answer, because they had forgotten to ask.

"Well, I guess they have set procedures," Zita said. "I'm sure it won't take too long, and they know that we're waiting. Has either of you thought about the funeral?"

"He was our child," Nicolai burst out. His voice was breaking up.

"I'm sorry," Zita said hastily. "I was only trying to help. I just thought we should make some decisions. And I thought that you might need someone to do that for you, as you have more than enough to deal with. How did the police treat you? Were they understanding? Did they treat you with respect?"

"They poked around and asked lots of questions about all sorts of things," Carmen said. "And Nicolai and I were kept in separate rooms, which I thought was horrible."

"But that's just procedure," Zita reassured her. "Rules that they have to follow in the event of sudden death and accidents. To find out exactly what happened."

"But we'd explained to them," Carmen said sulkily. "In detail. And still they said that we might have to go in again. To answer more questions after the autopsy. But they won't find anything. He was fit and healthy. He had that ear infection once but got over it quick enough. I told them that Tommy was healthy."

They sat in silence while eating Elsa's food. Nicolai was hungry, but he let it gnaw at him and only took a couple of mouthfuls. Afterward Zita went out into the yard and wandered around aimlessly, not knowing what to do. If there was anything, anything at all that could soothe the pain, he thought. Again and again he berated himself for not having built a fence.

Nicolai wanted them to leave, because he wanted to be alone. He wanted to grieve without onlookers. He left the house again around midnight and went back down to the pond. He sat at the end of the jetty and wept. He could barely resist the lure of the black water.

9

ELEVENTH OF AUGUST. Morning.

"I dreamed about death," she wailed. "He was right here in the room, and he was falling to pieces. All stained and rotten and messy, with long yellow nails. I've never seen anything so hideous in my life. He sat on the rug beside the bed all night, breathing. It was disgusting. I thought I could still smell him when I woke up—a kind of sweet, rotten smell. And something's bitten me on the thigh. Look, it's all red and starting to swell up."

"A wasp," Nicolai said, exhausted. "There's some lidocaine cream in the bathroom drawer. It should help a little."

"Haven't you slept?"

"No."

"Have you been drinking whiskey?"

"Yes."

"More than one?"

"Yes, and don't worry. I can do what I like with my life. If I want to go to hell, I'll go to hell."

Carmen stood there for a while, thinking she desperately wanted to say the right thing. She wanted to be good and to save him. Because that was what the situation called for. She had to put out the fire that was burning all around her. She saw the empty glass on the table and started to fret. To think that he was sitting here drinking on his own so early in the morning.

"It won't get any better if you're tired and hungry," she said. "It won't get any better if you're drunk. We don't need to numb ourselves; we have to get through this. And there are things we need to organize. The funeral and lots of other things. Listen to me, I'm trying to help!"

He didn't answer. Just sat there and played with the fringe on the blanket. His eyes were swollen from crying and his hair was a mess. She stood looking at him, not knowing what to say. So she said nothing, went into the kitchen, and put on the kettle. She had a life to live, after all. She needed air in her lungs, blood in her arms and legs. Things had to keep working. He called to her from the living room.

"Why do you think they want to examine the house?"

She went back out and fell into a chair. She licked her finger and brushed it over the bite, because she thought that spit might soothe it. That was right, wasn't it?

"Don't think about it anymore," she said in a comforting voice. "It's bad enough as it is, and you're only making it worse sitting here brooding. I don't know why they want to look at the house, but I guess they'll do what they like."

He pulled off the blanket and sent her a dark look. His eyes, which she normally thought were kind, were suddenly accusing.

"You didn't think Tommy was good enough," he said.

Carmen didn't recognize his voice. Again he showed a bitterness that only confused her.

"I've known it the whole time. Ever since we were at the hospital and the doctors came into the room with the bad news. I remember your face, your expression when you realized the truth. You'd had a baby, and you made a face."

Carmen looked at him across the table and scratched the red, now irritated bite. She stepped into the bathroom to get the cream.

"You weren't exactly clapping with joy, either," she countered. "And I can't help my feelings. I am the way I am. But you can't say that I didn't love him. Because I did. I loved my little Tommy. More than you know."

She blinked away her tears, moved by her own words. It was strange to be sitting here early in the morning with Nicolai, without Tommy crying or making a fuss or needing something. It was bizarrely quiet, as though time had stopped. The new day lay ahead of her, aching with a new and welcome freedom.

"They won't give up," Nicolai told her. "They're going to keep asking questions, because that's what they're like. What we've done and not done, what we were thinking. Did we love him and how much are we grieving? How deep is your grief?" he asked, looking at her with his wet green eyes.

She pulled herself up a bit and said she had told them all there was to tell. That she came out of the bathroom and saw that he wasn't there. And yes, it had taken awhile. Enough time for Tommy to toddle out of the house and across the yard down to the water.

"So," she said, looking at his drawn face, "they can call me in for questioning as many times as they like. They can ask questions and poke around for as long as they like, but I've got nothing more to tell them. I'm done."

But most of all, in the midst of it all, she wanted to be good. She wanted him to be on her side, at any price. She stood up and went over to the sofa, sat down on his knee, and kissed his tense and pale cheek.

"I know you don't like me saying it," she said, "but we can

49

have another baby sooner or later. Maybe a little girl. Margrete or Maria. You can decide."

"I don't want a little girl," Nicolai wailed. "I want Tommy. Now, right now!"

She stroked his hair with her delicate hand. "But you'll never get him back. Now we only have memories. You were a good dad, so be proud of that."

"What were you doing in the bathroom?" he asked all of a sudden. "Why did you leave him?"

She thought for a moment and then answered quickly. "Oh, I was just doing some washing. The door didn't even cross my mind. I'm really sorry. I was away for about five minutes, maybe, and he can get quite far in that time. But I won't let you blame me. And whether you like it or not, life goes on. We have to focus on the funeral now and make sure it's beautiful in the church."

He didn't want her on his lap. He pushed her off and down onto the sofa and ran his hands through his thin, straight hair.

"You don't leave a toddler on his own," he retorted. "Especially not one like Tommy. You could have called for me; I could have watched him while you did the washing. You never learn! It wasn't the first time he'd managed to get out of the house. So just admit you made a mistake and that you're irresponsible, because that's what you are."

"The washing was just as important as your bikes. And in any case, I'm the one who does all the work. You just played with him in the evenings and had fun."

"Which of us is going to call the funeral people?" he asked.

"Pappa Zita will do that," she replied. "He's going to call Sentrum. He'll explain everything to them, that we have to wait for the body. That is, if you can't face doing it yourself. It's good we've got Dad. I don't know how we would get through this without him. So, do you want a cup of tea? The water's boiling; I can hear it."

He said no. Instead he went to the cupboard and got out a bottle of whiskey. He poured another dram, lifted the glass, and drank it down.

"You can't drink at seven in the morning," she exclaimed, horrified.

"I can do exactly what I want. No one is going to tell me how to grieve."

10

SEJER LIKED TO have someone else breathing in the room, even if it was only a dog. Every now and then, Frank's paws quivered as he ran across the fields of his dreams chasing his prey, a cat or a rabbit perhaps. Still alone, Sejer thought, and stretched his long, sinewy body. That's what my life has become. It's not what I had planned, but it's what I got. He flipped the comforter to one side and put a foot down on the floor. He had often thought about getting a single bed, because that would have made more space in the already Spartan room. But thoughts had never led to action, because sometimes in his imagination Elise was still lying there sleeping beside him, silently in the empty space. This gave him gentle, if temporary, solace. But Elise had been entrusted to the earth and darkness, and that made him melancholy. He went over to the window and pulled the curtain to one side. He looked out at the sleeping town that would shortly wake up, a glittering bowl of light between the deep blue hills. Soon it would stir to life again, flare into action. The river was a leaden ribbon, stubbornly pushing its steady way to the sea. He gave Frank an affectionate pat on the head and went into the bathroom. He stared at himself in the mirror and met his own searching eyes. They were as gray as slate, Elise had once said when they were young. No, he wasn't at all dizzy, not today. His head was crystal clear and his thoughts were free and light. It was, as he had long hoped, finally over. It had to be over now. What a fuss it had all been. Frank made his way into the kitchen and over to his water dish and sleepily slurped up some water left from the day before.

"What do you reckon, Frank?" he asked the dog. "Do we have a murder on our hands? Something's not right; I'd put my money on it. I bet you two pork chops. Even though you're fat enough as it is."

Frank padded back to the bathroom and stopped on the threshold, studying his master standing there with a razor in his hand. On the walls, blue and white tiles with dolphins jumped. "Laughable" was his comment on the dolphins, but once upon a time they had been perfect, because there was something joyous about them, something inspiring.

"Do you think they managed to sleep last night?" he asked the dog. "My guess is that she did and he didn't. I hope Snorrason finds something definite. It's possible, after all. Nothing gets by that man. Maybe his little body is full of toxins, who knows? We'll get to the bottom of this, is that a deal? You've got a good nose and I've got my suspicions." The dog grunted a reply and collapsed on the floor. Sejer finished his morning ablutions and got dressed, knotting his dark blue silk tie carefully. Many years ago, Elise had embroidered a small cherry with a green stalk on it. It was the sort of thing she had always liked to do.

I'm sure they'll be up by now, he thought. Wandering around in despair. Looking to the heavens, praying fervently to God, and cursing fate. But no matter where they look, they won't find an answer or any soothing words. Carmen Zita is desperate, Nicolai silent and morose. That was how he imagined they would be. They were so different. We humans are put to so many tests, it doesn't bear thinking about, he mused. Losing a child after only sixteen months. Having to haul the dead child out of the water, panic and fear tearing at your body. He put Frank on his leash and went out to greet the new day, crossing the parking lot to the small path through the woods. Other people and animals had been there before them and Frank sniffed around and searched for a trophy as always. As he walked, he enjoyed the strengthening light and lush vegetation. Bracken, thistles, and cow parsley, willow weed and mugwort, which sometimes made his eyes and nose run. Once the dog had done what he needed to, Sejer turned and walked back to the apartment building where he lived on the top floor. He picked up the paper that was lying on the mat and looked for the modest report, which he found at the back of the news section. Sixteen-month-old boy found drowned in Damtjern. Mouth-to-mouth was given immediately but any attempt to resuscitate failed, and the boy was declared dead after about an hour.

He brushed his teeth, put on his leather jacket, and picked up his briefcase from the desk. So far there were only a couple of documents concerning Tommy's death. He asked Frank if he wanted to go to work. The dog ran to the door and sat there whining.

"We're going out to Granfoss," Sejer said, "and you're coming with us."

Skarre swallowed a jelly bean. The sugar surged through his veins, making him more alert.

"You've got no shame," he said with a smile.

"I'm not going to harass them," Sejer said. "Just a follow-up call to show that we care. To hear how they coped with the first terrible night. There are some upsetting aspects to the job, I agree. But if little Tommy was thrown in the pond on purpose, then someone is going to pay."

"Absolutely," Skarre agreed. "If I know you, you won't let it go. Why are you so certain something is wrong?"

"Well," Sejer began, "strictly speaking it was you who started it all, and I'm just following up on what you told me when we were standing down there by the pond. But Carmen Zita is obviously nervous. And she is not overwhelmed by grief. Her tears feel more like anxiety about what might lie in store."

"I refused to let them do an autopsy," Sejer said, once they were in the car. "I mean, when Elise died. Couldn't bear the thought of it. I didn't want those images in my head. It's so brutal, opening up the body and emptying out all the organs."

"You refused?" Skarre repeated in surprise. "Can you do that?"

"Yes," Sejer said. "In many cases you can. The body belongs to the family. But not in the event of a suspicious death. Then it's we who decide. But you know how it happened. It wasn't exactly a secret that she died of liver cancer."

His openness astonished Skarre. Sejer was not usually generous when it came to talking about personal things, particularly when it came to his late wife, Elise, or anything to do with her tragic death. Even though it was a long time ago now. Skarre knew to value this intimacy and thought that it meant something—trust, for instance. They had known each other for many years, after all. They could confide in each other. The older and the younger, a kind of warm, sociable partnership that had borne fruit in the form of numerous solved cases. The two men were famous in the district for their style and integrity.

"It's early," he said. "They might not be up yet."

"They probably haven't slept," Sejer replied. "It wouldn't surprise me if they were sitting there waiting. The fate of a liar, you know, expecting to be caught at any moment."

Carmen Zita was wearing tiny denim shorts and a top with Snow White and the Seven Dwarfs on the front, thus confirming Sejer's impression that she was still a child. When she saw both of them on the steps outside, she backed up a bit and put a hand to her head.

"Why are you here?" she asked. "Is there any news about Tommy? Already, after only one night?"

Sejer held out his hand and she took it, but her handshake was reluctant and without force.

"Are you going to ask us in?" Sejer suggested calmly. Carmen reversed into the hall.

"Yes, of course. Come on in. Dad will be here soon," she added, as if she wanted to say that her time was limited and they were not particularly welcome. It was rather inconvenient in fact, and she really wanted them to leave. They could feel her reluctance, and she kept her distance.

"He's going to help us with the funeral," she explained. "We don't have much money. We've got practically nothing," she sighed, and shrugged with her palms up. "Dad's trying to find someone to cover for us at Zita Quick. We can't exactly work now, either of us, can we? After what's happened. Follow me; let's go into the kitchen. Let's get this over and done with. It's starting to bother me."

She walked in front of them through the house. She sat down at the kitchen table and pointed to the empty chairs beside Nicolai with a resigned expression. Then she put her hand to her eyes to wipe away a tear, as they had started to fall again.

"Where is he now?" she asked. "Have they finished the autopsy? Is he lying in a drawer in the morgue?"

Sejer nodded. "Yes, yes, he is. And it will no doubt take some time before everything is sorted."

"But we want to have the funeral as soon as possible," Nicolai said, clearly anxious. "How long do you think we'll have to wait?"

"That depends on the autopsy," Skarre explained. "And on if they find anything. We promise to keep you informed."

"But can we start planning?" Carmen asked. "There's so much that has to be decided. Music and flowers and all sorts of things. He's going to be buried at Møller Church. Can we choose a plot? There are some lovely birch trees on the slope up there. And we've got a plot there from before. Or will we be allocated something randomly?"

"I guess that you will be allocated a plot," Skarre said. "But it will be beautiful, I'm sure of that. Tommy will be given the best place."

"My sister Louisa is buried under the birch trees," Carmen told them. "It would be nice if they could be near each other; they're related, after all. Aunty Louisa," she said with a smile. "I'm definitely going to ask the priest if we can have our wish. I mean, they have to listen to us, don't they?"

"Do that," Sejer said. "I'm glad to hear that you're getting help with the funeral, because they are expensive. You'll get some financial help, but I'm not sure how much, as it's based on need. But every little bit helps. You must take good care of each other through all this," he said in a kind voice. "Otherwise it will be an incredibly lonely time, believe me."

"What do you know about grief?" Nicolai said angrily.

"Everything," was Sejer's curt reply. "Both personal and professional, and what's more, it is part of my job to look after people. No two people grieve alike; you must remember that. Now, there's something else I'd like to ask," he said, changing the subject. "If you don't find it too painful to answer. Did Tommy have a favorite between the two of you? I mean, was he closer to one of you?"

"Tommy was a daddy's boy," Nicolai said firmly. "And I was proud of that."

"Yes, it's always like that, isn't it?" Carmen said. "Daddy's so great. Because he's not there most of the time. So there's even more excitement when he does finally come home again in the evening. And he's still got the energy to play, whereas I've been holding down the fort all day. And you know what, in the end you run out of ideas. Tommy was also very stubborn. It wasn't always easy to keep him happy. But then I'm a daddy's girl," she said, "so I guess I'll just have to accept the fact that Nicolai was more fun."

"Can I ask one more thing?" Sejer pushed. "Would we be welcome at Tommy's funeral?"

"Yes, of course," Carmen said. "Of course, you're welcome to come to the church. But please come in a normal car. And neither of you can be in uniform," she added, nodding at Skarre. "I don't want that. People will talk. You know how it is; we live in a small place."

Sejer promised to do as they wished.

"Please let us know if you would like to talk to a psychologist," he offered in a kindly manner.

Nicolai shook his head. "There's not a lot to say. We've lost our child and we're sad. What can they do to help? It's just rubbish. And don't give me all that talk about group therapy," he said. "Sitting in a circle and sharing your innermost thoughts and feelings, no way. As I see it, grief is a private thing. And even if there are others in the same situation, Tommy was special. In every way. And we're the only ones who've lost a boy like that."

"Of course," Sejer placated him. "But you are also allowed to change your minds, so just let me know. And promise me not to underestimate other people. There's a lot to be said for experience, even if you don't appreciate that now. A lot of people have been there before, and sometimes it's good to lean on others. There, I've said my bit. And we'll let you know as soon as the body is released."

Carmen followed them out. She stood in the doorway, hesitating.

"Does the fact that you've come here mean something?" she asked. "Be honest."

Sejer put his hand on her arm. "It simply means that we care," he said, "and are doing all that we can in Tommy's best interest."

11

MARIAN ZITA'S FAST-FOOD café was in the pedestrian zone between the square and 7-Eleven. It had red awnings over the windows and a sign above the door read ZITA QUICK. There were twenty settings inside, and the whole place was saturated with the smell of fried food and spices. A girl wearing red nylon overalls and a hairnet was standing behind the counter.

"Can I help you?" she said. "Do you want to eat in? Or take out? The chairs in here are quite comfortable, but the ones outside are wrought iron, so we get quite a few complaints. Just so you know. So, how can I help you?" she said again. Her cheeks were flushed, perhaps because Skarre was a handsome sight in his immaculate uniform, with his blond curls under the black cap.

"Is something wrong?"

Sejer nodded to one of the tables at the back of the café. "Could be," he said seriously. "Can you sit down for a couple of minutes?"

She nodded, came around from behind the counter, and walked toward them. She's about the same age as Carmen, Sejer thought, or maybe a little older. Certainly no more than twenty-two.

"Um, well," she stammered, "I just thought, is it to do with Carmen and Nicolai's baby?"

Sejer gave her a reassuring look. She was wearing a locket around her neck, which might have a photo of her sweetheart inside. She sat there playing with it now, obviously nervous and anxious.

"Yes," he replied. "We just want to talk to you a little about what happened up at Damtjern. You see, that's what we do when someone dies. Especially if it's a child."

"But it was an accident, wasn't it?" she said. "He fell off the jetty? That's what Pappa Zita said when he called yesterday—that Tommy had wandered out of the kitchen and down to the pond. I almost couldn't understand what he was saying. He was so upset, and I've never heard him like that before. It was scary. He's always so big and strong, but he was crying like a baby. I had to ask him to repeat himself a few times, and it was difficult to know what to say. To be honest, I don't even remember what I said. I was lost for words. I was pretty useless, really."

"How well do you know Carmen and Nicolai?" Sejer asked.

She looked at them, one and then the other, her eyes as brown as horse chestnuts. She seemed to be honest and sincere.

"Not very well. I'm just a cover," she explained. "I work when someone's ill or on vacation, that sort of thing. And I'm working today because of Tommy. I mean, I speak to them sometimes, and I really feel for them right now. I don't even know where to begin. Tommy's a good boy, even if he is a bit different. There's something good about children like that. They steal a piece of your heart."

"That's a nice thing to say," Sejer remarked. "If only everyone could see it like that, things would be a lot better. Do you know what they were like as parents? They're so young. What about Nicolai? What kind of father was he? Tell me what you know."

"He was over the moon," she said. "Never angry or anything like that. He really loved Tommy just the way he was."

"And what about Carmen?" he probed.

"Well, Carmen," she started, and then paused. "I think basi-

61

cally it bothered her. And I can understand that, since it must be really hard. Or maybe she was just embarrassed. She certainly never talked about it. She never talked about Tommy at all, which I thought was a bit weird. Most people love to talk about their children, but she wasn't like that. If anyone mentioned that he was different, she immediately changed the subject, to the weather or something like that. Perhaps I shouldn't be telling you, but it's the truth. I've thought about it quite a lot. Having a child that you constantly have to explain to everyone else must be so hard and exhausting. You can't ever get away from it. It's always there, just think about it. Different and slow and in need of help. Different today and different every day for the rest of their lives."

She sighed, paused, and shifted her position in the chair. As if she was suddenly uncomfortable that she had just admitted this. But they were from the police and she automatically felt she had to tell the truth at all costs. It just seemed to flow out of her.

"People could see he wasn't right," she continued, "and I think Carmen hated having to answer all the questions. But I'm sure she loved him as well, in her own way. Don't you think? I mean, people come to love their children, no matter what."

"Yes, that's what we believe too," Skarre assured her. "So, you'll be getting a lot of shifts now. And I guess no one knows when they'll be back at work?"

"Yes, I'll do all I can to help, and I need the money. It's just awful. I don't know what to say, really. To think that things like this happen, it's horrible."

"Have you ever looked after him? Babysat or anything like that?"

"Yes, actually," she said. "Just once. I went to their house up at Damtjern. It was Pappa Zita's fiftieth and they were having a big party for him at that place at Granfoss. They thought it would be best if Tommy didn't go. There was a band and all that, and they thought that maybe there would be too much noise for him."

Sejer sat for a while thinking.

"What's your name?" he asked after a pause.

"Elisabeth," she replied.

"Elisabeth. Right. Do you mind if I ask you a personal question?"

"Of course. I'm OK with that," she said with a slight smile. She adjusted her hairnet and folded her hands on the table, waiting like a schoolgirl.

"Do you have children?"

"No, I don't have children. I don't even have a boyfriend."

Skarre looked at her intently. "You mean right now, today, you don't have a boyfriend?"

"Yes, because we broke up on Friday," she said and let out a light, tinkling laugh. Her laughter was cheering in the midst of all the sadness.

"But," Sejer pushed, "if you were expecting a baby, that is, you and a possible partner—which you don't have at the moment, but still, a boyfriend—and the doctor did an amnio, as they do on some women these days when they think there is a risk. Imagine that you were told that the baby you were carrying had Down syndrome. Would you have an abortion? Or would you choose to have the baby? Sorry to be so intrusive, and I understand if you don't want to answer. I'm just curious."

Elisabeth was silent. They could see that she really was pondering it. It was a difficult question.

"Be honest," Skarre interjected. "I mean, be as honest as you can. We're not going to judge you, you can be sure of that."

"I hope I never have to make that choice," she said in the end. "And I know it's awful, but I think I would have an abortion. I mean, it's a choice that affects the rest of your life."

Sejer and Skarre nodded.

"What about Carmen and Nicolai. Did they know that Tommy had Down syndrome beforehand?"

"No, I'm fairly sure they didn't. If they did, they kept it secret, but we would have been able to tell. No one talked about it after he was born either; it was only after a while that it started to come out. But Pappa Zita was really upset about it. He was worried about Carmen, which is understandable. Because they only have her now. They lost her twin sister nineteen years ago, if you didn't already know. And I'm sure all that's coming up again now. Jesus, I can't imagine all that tragedy." She wrapped the chain and pendant around her fingers and looked very dejected.

"Thank you, Elisabeth," Sejer said. "And now we'd like you to make a burger for us as we haven't eaten since breakfast. And we'd like you to do it with love, because then it always tastes better."

She laughed and pushed back the chair. Then she disappeared behind the counter again. Perhaps she was relieved that the conversation was over, but they both noticed a wrinkle on her forehead, as though she was worried about something she'd said. In case she had weakened someone's case. If there was a case. While she made the food, Sejer went over to look at all the certificates hanging on the wall. The town's best burger 2006, the town's best burger 2007. And so on, in a long line. And then a brass plaque: OPEN 24 HOURS.

"What would you have done?" Skarre asked him, while they waited for their burgers. "With a baby like that."

Sejer thought about it. The smell of burgers wafted into the room.

"I would have had to listen to Elise and taken her feelings into consideration. No matter what we say about equality, it's the mother who's closest. But deep down, I think I would have hoped she'd have an abortion. Oh yes—now you're going to give me a hard time, but to be fair it gives me a taste of my own medicine. And yes, I think choices like that are horrendous. And we have to make so many in life. By nature we tend to die before our children, and it must be so hard to know you're going to die before a child that will always need help. What about you? Would you see it as God's will and therefore feel obliged to keep a child with Down syndrome?"

"Good question," Skarre said. "You don't make it any easier for me. And ultimately, I think I would also choose not to have the child. But not without an ocean of bad conscience."

12

Morning.

The summer heat continued, but a powerful thunderstorm was brewing, and heavy black clouds loomed in the sky. Sejer liked a good storm, the intense drama of nature, and he was sick and tired of the heat that had dominated the summer. It was stifling and made him heavy-headed. He longed for something fresher, like lower temperatures and a cleansing downpour.

The pathologist, Bardy Snorrason, had worked in the institute for more than thirty years. He spoke Norwegian with a wonderful accent and the rolling sharp consonants so characteristic of Icelanders. He was a handsome red-haired chap who commanded considerable authority and was very thorough. Sejer had often put his trust in his intricate and revealing finds in both major and less important cases. In short, Snorrason was the best and always to be found in his office. There he was, hunched over a pile of papers in deep concentration, his glasses perched on the end of his nose. He was interested in the small boy's body and had written a very detailed report. He could never get used to it. A small dead child was tragic every time, and a melancholy had settled on him that could last a long while.

"No point in being modest in this profession," Sejer said somberly. "So here I am, hoping to get an answer. And I know you normally prioritize in order of conscience. Women and children first, isn't that so?"

Snorrason pointed to a chair. "Yes, I've been busy. And already we can ascertain that he was alive when he fell in the pond. There is a lot of water in his lungs, and dear God, the poor little mite fought against death. He'd drawn lots of water down into his lungs in a panic. I have also done a number of tests. But I'm afraid you'll just have to be patient and wait for those results, as there are plenty in line ahead of us. What about you, have you found anything? Have you got any more out of the parents?

"No," Sejer said. "They just repeat the same story. Carmen Zita is insistent when it comes to the sequence of events. But she's uncertain and a bit vague in her explanation. She says, "Yes, I'm not sure, but I think I was cleaning the fish," which has since proved to be true. But I still feel uneasy. You know how it is, intuition, and I felt it from the outset. She likes to perform and is pretty artificial to begin with, so it's easy to take what she says with a grain of salt anyway. But you know, it's almost like a smell or a particular mood. And over the years, like you, I've become a wily old fox."

Snorrason took off his glasses and popped them on his knee. He rubbed his eyes as though he was tired. And perhaps he was; he wasn't getting any younger. But retiring was out of the question, even though he was well over sixty. The greater part of his time was spent teaching younger minds who would eventually take over from him when he did step back. He got up and walked over to the green filing cabinet, took out the preliminary report, and started to read.

"Tommy Nicolai Zita. Age, sixteen months. Well-nourished and apparently healthy in every possible way, with the obvious exception of Down syndrome. The syndrome is a genetic disorder, not an illness, which results in secondary complications and deficiencies over time. But he had no heart problems, as a good many people with Down syndrome do; he was fit and healthy. And there is no reason to believe that he would not have done well in life, despite his disabilities. No visible traumas to the body. No wounds, no breaks, no bruises, no internal bleeding. Toxins? Don't know, too early to say. Samples have been taken and sent to the lab, so we're waiting for answers."

He gave Sejer a grave look. "Poor little man. Drowning is not a pleasant way to go and it takes some time. The water burns your lungs like fire and it's incredibly painful. So, you're open to the eventuality that something criminal may have occurred?"

"Yes," Sejer replied. "There's something about Miss Carmen Zita that unnerves me. She is strong and stubborn and insistent. She weeps buckets, but it feels forced. I'm sure you know what I mean. Something's not right."

Snorrason put the papers away. "Do you mean a lack of grief?"

"Well," Sejer started, then paused. "One has to be careful when judging another person's grief. There's no set formula, no exact science. Everyone grieves in his or her own way. Some people want to move on quickly, whereas others want to hold on to it, wrap it around them. But she has an odd manner, and I don't believe her. Like I said, she cries at the drop of a hat, constant tears. When I ask probing questions, she gets angry and defensive, fights tooth and nail to keep me at bay. The boy's father, Nicolai, is more reserved. He really does seem to be shaken to the core. So if there is anything fishy, it is perhaps her work alone. That's my current theory. But it's worth nothing without proof. To be honest, I hope that you don't find anything that confirms my suspicions. But he was different, after all. Could that be a motive in itself?"

"What you fear could well be hard to prove," Snorrason said in a serious voice. "So far I've found nothing to support your assumptions. Sad but true. Of course, there are things we don't pick up on, even if we're both on the ball. And there are lots of unrecorded cases. A certain share of all accidents are disguised killings, and of course some people get away with it. But there's no point in getting upset. We do as best we can, both you and I. And as this is a little boy, we have to be even more aware of our responsibility and keep our eyes peeled for any irregularities."

He put his glasses back on.

"To drown a child on purpose and to stand there watching while he or she struggles in the water requires a degree of madness," he said. "To be blunt, it requires a cold heart. So, what do you think in relation to the mother? She's only nineteen. Is she capable of such brutality?"

"Too early to say," Sejer replied. "We've only spoken a couple of times."

Snorrason rolled his chair back to his desk to indicate that he had a lot to do.

"I'll contact you as soon as I hear from the lab," he said.

13

DID SHE STAND there and watch? Sejer thought miserably.

Did she carry him down to the water while Nicolai was busy with some old bicycle? Did she walk through the grass and along the jetty, throw him into the water, and watch him flail and thrash around? Did she watch with dead eyes and an icy heart? I couldn't even drown a rat, Sejer thought. It would repulse me. The fear, screams, cramps, and panic. Whether it was from a human or an animal, it was just as bad.

He put on a Monica Zetterlund CD, found a pouch of tobacco in a kitchen drawer, and started to roll a fat cigarette. He only smoked one in the evening; he was a man of moderation. And he had to have a whiskey after all the day's endeavors, a generous dram to warm his heart. Frank lay at his feet, his breathing shallow, his little pink tongue hanging out the corner of his mouth. Elise, he thought, and looked up at the wall where a photograph of her beamed down at him. The whiskey made him sentimental, and the nicotine gave him a head rush and made him slightly dizzy. Elise, can you see me now? Can you see that we're doing OK, Frank and I? But you know, there are always difficult days in a person's life, days that we can't avoid. There is no life without resistance, no days without worry, no years without pain, no nights without loneliness. There is anguish, dark thoughts, and sparkling hope in every person's life. And we switch between these all the time, he thought. Everyone is caught in a storm throughout his or her entire life. Carmen and Nicolai were in the middle of the storm. He took a drag on the cigarette and drew the smoke down into his lungs. He was still a bit fuzzy in the head, light and floaty, and outside himself. Dusk was falling outside, night was on the way, and he welcomed it like an old friend. He heard the rumble of thunder in the distance and it slowly rolled closer. I'm actually quite happy now, he mused, and took a sip of the warming whiskey. I'm certainly fairly content with life. If only my health doesn't deteriorate, if only this dizziness doesn't take over completely. Why should I get away with it? Not that I've ever really thought like that, we humans are exposed to so much. Every day someone is knocked off their feet, thrown brutally and mercilessly to the ground, and abandoned without hope. Sooner or later, fate will catch up with me. Hey you, fate will say, you've got away with it for too long; now it's your turn. Time for you to get up and fight, because it's now or never.

Frank padded out into the kitchen to drink some water. Sejer could hear the slurping from where he was in the living room. It was a relaxing sound. The whiskey warmed the pit of his stomach and he felt at ease. Not surprising that people turned to alcohol, he thought, it helped against most things. Against pain, despair, sorrow, worry, and anguish. Against all kinds of obstacles and difficulties. The alcohol flooded his veins and made him feel warm and light. He got up and went over to the window, looking down at the town he loved so much. The river with all its bridges, the beautifully lit brewery, the elegant church. And the busy port, where all the imported cars came into the country before rolling out onto the Norwegian roads: Hondas, Toyotas, and Mercedes in endless lines. Trains on their way into and out of the station; boats on the river with lanterns lit. He put his glass down on the kitchen counter and went to the bathroom. He brushed his teeth and went to bed. Frank trotted in behind him and lay down on the rug by the bed as he always did, and they lay there together awake for about fifteen minutes. Then they dozed off and soon fell into a deep sleep free of worries.

14

FIFTEENTH OF AUGUST. Afternoon at Granfoss.

Carmen walked around with a large garbage bag and picked up toys from all the nooks and crannies: a teddy bear, a pacifier, a teething ring, a yellow plastic tractor, and a red fire engine. Things that boys like to play with. Wind-up toys and soft toys, Lego blocks and Playmobil animals. Then she went to the chest of drawers in the bedroom. She pulled out the drawers and started to put the baby clothes in the bag. Her movements were quick and efficient; she did not hesitate for a moment. The clothes were folded and put away.

"We can take it to the Salvation Army shop," she said in a very practical manner. Nicolai stood in the doorway and watched her wide-eyed. Repugnance and rage churned inside him. He couldn't believe what was happening—that she was tidying Tommy out of the house and getting rid of every single little thing before he was even in the ground.

"Surely you could wait with that," he objected.

But Carmen wouldn't listen. She continued with what she was doing.

"The funeral people will be coming soon," she said, "and everything's such a mess. And I don't like being reminded. His things are everywhere. And he's never coming back."

"You said we could have another baby," he remarked. "You said we could maybe have a girl. Have you changed your mind? We could use his clothes then, and the toys would come in handy. The carriage, the crib, everything. What are you thinking?"

She carried on putting the clothes in the bag. Most of them were blue or white, trousers, tops and overalls, mittens and hats. She said nothing in reply to his comment, just gritted her teeth and completely ignored him. I am the mother, she thought furiously; I am the one who decides.

Nicolai tried to pull himself together. He felt like a coward, because he couldn't confront her with all his feelings raging inside. Deep down he felt an inexplicable fear, roaring in the depths of his being, that something was wrong. He wasn't sure about what had actually happened on August 10 and his imagination was running wild. Tommy, he thought, my little man. We'll meet again in a better world. He allowed himself these thoughts, even though he wasn't a believer. Because the alternative, that he was gone forever, was simply unbearable. For sixteen months, he had been a devoted father. He had lifted the boy up and thrown him in the air so he screeched with delight, thrown balls and sung songs for him at night. He had felt the warmth of his body against his cheek, the soft, soapy smell of a freshly bathed baby. In his eyes, Tommy was the best little boy in the world, full of joy and delight, despite the Down syndrome.

"Maybe we could sell the carriage," Carmen said and glanced over at him. "I'm sure we'd get quite a bit for it, since it's as good as new."

"But the carriage was a present from your parents," he said, horrified. "Get a grip, Carmen; what do you think they'd say?"

"Cross that bridge when we get to it," was her reply. "And Dad will understand. And in any case, it's blue. And next time we might have a little girl." She bent down over the garbage bag again and continued to fill it with clothes. It was almost full. Before, when she stood like that with her neat little bum in the air, it produced an explosion of burning desire. Now he felt nothing except deep antipathy. She straightened up and paused. She brushed the platinum hair away from her eyes and put her hands on her hips with that elegant tilt to her hips that he normally liked.

"Maybe we should cremate him," she said. "Then we'll get an urn and we could maybe take it home with us. Then he'd be here with us; what do you think?"

Nicolai looked at her in disbelief. He felt himself wobbling and had to lean against the door frame. Burn poor little Tommy to ash? No, there was no way he'd allow that.

"He's going to be buried," he said in desperation. "Don't say things like that."

Up went her bum again and she carried on with the bottom drawer.

"Oh well, just thought I'd mention it," she said. "I don't think we should cremate him either. I just wanted to know what you thought. I mean, God, we have to talk about things, don't we? Don't be so sensitive!"

"You don't care what I think in any case," he said. Tears welled up and stung his eyes.

"I don't understand you," he said after a while. "Put the bag down, we're going out. Let's go to Stranda. I need a swim."

She continued emptying the bottom drawer, wanting to get it finished. But the thought of going to Stranda appealed to her, although first she had to go to the bathroom. They might run into someone and she wanted to look her best. She was concerned about that. And now, especially when things were so hard, she had to keep up appearances.

They walked hand in hand down the path like a young couple in love. There had been a big thunderstorm in the night and it had rained heavily afterward. The clouds had cleared again and everything felt new and fresh, and the heat they had had for so long had returned. The sun burned down relentlessly from a hazy sky. He held her hand tightly, so hard, in fact, that she whimpered. He had put his trunks on under his jeans and the thought of a long swim worked wonders.

"Do you think they'll have finished the autopsy by now?" Carmen asked. She gave his hand a little squeeze, as though she wanted to take the edge off this painful question.

"They promised they'd call," Nicolai replied, "and we haven't heard anything yet. I don't know. There's nothing to find anyway. I wish it wasn't necessary, but there's no point in protesting. They've got all the power."

Now it was he who squeezed her hand.

"Sorry," he said all of a sudden.

Carmen looked up at him and gave him a squeeze back. She was wearing her ring with a red stone in it, and he felt the sharp edge hard against his palm.

"Why are you saying sorry?"

Nicolai had started to walk faster, and she had to trot a little to keep up.

"I know that I'm being difficult and mean," he said. "I know that I'm complaining. But at the moment I'm just so sad. And I don't want another child, just so you know. There's no point in talking about a replacement, because it's not possible."

Carmen shook her head in exasperation; now it was her turn to be sad.

"You'll learn to love another one just as much," she said. "I know you. You're so kind. You're the world's best dad. And we can wait a bit, anyway, until everything has gone back to normal. We're in the middle of it all right now and that makes it difficult to think. Maybe after the funeral we'll be able to move on. Pappa

Zita says that the funeral is a kind of turning point. I hope we get a place for him under the birch trees beside Louisa."

They walked in silence the rest of the way.

When they got to Stranda, Carmen sat down on the warm sand and Nicolai took off his jeans. He walked slowly down to the water, waded out, and then dived in. He was a strong swimmer and kept good speed straight out from the shore, with strong, determined strokes. She followed his progress.

"Don't go too far," she called to him. "It's best to stick to the shore, and I can't save you if you get cramps."

She forced a little laughter, but it felt uncomfortable in her mouth. Nicolai didn't answer; he just kept on swimming with steady strokes. Carmen could see a tanker farther out. The red hull was visible on the horizon. She kept her eye on Nicolai the entire time. He was now so far away that she started to get anxious. And he showed no sign of turning back. Terrible thoughts flooded her mind: maybe he couldn't face any more, and he was leaving it all behind. She stood up and shaded her eyes, catching sight of his head in the gentle waves, bobbing up and down like a cork. She started to dig in the wet sand, trying to make a sandcastle. But she wasn't any good at it, and the castle kept collapsing. As a child, she had come here often with her father. He was as strong as an ox and had carried her on his shoulders all the way, and she rocked and felt like she was on a boat. Then he'd lifted her down onto the sand and answered all her questions. Why don't fish drown? Well, her father told her, they get air through their gills. A fine profusion of tiny bubbles of oxygen. And just think how fast they move in the water. Everything that lives in this world needs air. Yes, her father was always on her side. No matter what happened, he was her mentor and her servant and he made her happy. She looked out at the water again to see if Nicolai had turned. But he hadn't, so she started to shout.

"Nicolai, you idiot, come back or I'll go home! I didn't manage to save Tommy. And I won't be able to save you!"

Finally he came to his senses, turned back, and swam toward the shore. She sighed with relief. She felt her body relax and started to build her little sandcastle again with eager hands. She managed to build a tower and dig a moat to channel in the water. She was delighted with her work, beaming up at Nicolai when he came out of the water.

"You scared me," she said later as she took his hand.

"Why?" he asked. "I'm a good swimmer. I'm best in the water and you know that."

He looked over the small sandcastle but was not particularly impressed, and she was hurt that he didn't even make a friendly comment. As they walked back, she was silent for a while. She had her turquoise sandals on. One of the straps was beginning to rub; they were not good to walk in. She knew that she would get a blister that would then burst and become a sore so she would have to use a bandage. Stupid damn shoes, she thought and got herself wound up.

"People will think you've wet yourself," she said with a little smile. There were dark patches on Nicolai's jeans from the wet trunks he still had on underneath. But he didn't care; he just kept walking. He wanted to get home again. He wanted to go down into the dim cellar where he could be alone.

"Don't walk so fast," Carmen complained. "I've got a blister."

15

SEVENTEENTH OF AUGUST. Morning at Møllergata 4.

His name was Felipe Marian Zita and he came from Barcelona, but his wife Elsa was as blond and blue-eyed as a Norwegian fjord. Zita himself was dark and olive-skinned. One of Sejer's first questions, given Carmen's almost white hair, was whether he really was her biological father.

"Genetics is a complex area," he said, "and it certainly played a trick on us. Carmen's tow-colored hair was quite a surprise. Many people have asked before you," he added. "You're in good company. But please, sit down, sit down. Elsa has made some coffee. And I've just spoken to Carmen, because she calls every day. She said that she's having bad dreams, which isn't surprising given what's happened. Lots of nightmares, recurring bad dreams. Nicolai is devastated and I'm really worried about him. He's such a sensitive boy. Carmen is coping better. She's strong, that girl, takes after me. I'm not sure what you're after, but we can certainly have a chat. I'm sure you have your reasons. And we don't go against the system, because that's not who we are. We're humble folk."

Zita was obviously nervous and he talked a lot and fast. But this was perhaps due to his Mediterranean temperament, Sejer thought. It was hard to stop him once he had started.

"Sit yourselves down. Elsa's just coming with the coffee, if you've got time."

Sejer and Skarre thanked him and settled among the colorful, bright cushions.

"Carmen will definitely have another child," Zita said. "And as soon as she can, if I know her right. But Nicolai thinks otherwise. He no doubt wants to wait awhile. He says that Tommy can't be replaced. But that's not what we want, that's not the point."

He got up and took some cups and saucers out of a cupboard and then sat back down at the table. The living room was obviously influenced by his Mediterranean background. Dark, heavy furniture, tapestries on the wall, potted plants in the windows. A carved wooden rocking horse with full saddle and bridle in leather. Tommy probably sat on that many a time, Sejer reflected sadly. He admired the modern chandelier with hundreds of cut-glass pieces that sparkled in the light from the window.

"And is it true that everyone calls you Pappa Zita?" Sejer inquired.

"Yes," said Zita, as he sipped his coffee. "It was Carmen who started calling me that, when she was quite small. And then everyone started to call me Pappa, which I like. I'm happy to be everyone's papa. Especially Nicolai, as he lost both his parents in a light-aircraft accident. They flew a Cessna straight into a storm—maybe you heard. And I'm a dad to everyone who works at Zita Quick. I've trained them all, and they're good. Perhaps people don't realize it, but working in a fast-food restaurant is a demanding job. And we have a fantastic reputation to live up to. Every day we have to deliver the very best. And we're the only ones in the area who are open twenty-four hours a day. So that means lots of employees, high wage costs. But it's good business. Very good business," he concluded.

Elsa nodded. She was incredibly reserved. She studied Sejer and Skarre, her blue eyes full of doubt and suspicion.

"Why are you here?" she asked with a sharp edge to her voice.

"It's a sudden death," Sejer explained. "Conversations like this are part of the procedure."

"That's what you say to everyone," she said, her voice now bitter. "Just routine, you say. But I don't see how we can be of any help. No wrong has been done. Just so that's clear, because I know what you're thinking. That's why you're here, and I can't bear the thought that you're here to poke around in our lives."

Sejer blew on his coffee and took a small sip. "Yes, we say that to everyone," he said, unruffled, "because it's the truth. Tell me what you thought about the pond, the fact that it was so close to the house. Did it worry you?"

"Yes," Zita replied. "We worried a lot. Water can be so alluring. But Tommy was still small, and we thought we had plenty of time. I mean, of course we'd thought about putting up a fence around the house. With a latched gate. But we never got around to it; then suddenly it was too late, because he'd started walking. I feel so sorry for Carmen and Nicolai. I don't have words."

Skarre put his cup down on its saucer with a clinking of porcelain. "How did Carmen react when it became clear that Tommy had Down syndrome?"

"Oh, she took it in stride," Zita said. "I think you could say that. Don't you think so, Elsa, she took it in stride?"

"Yes," she agreed. "They both took it in stride. As my husband said, Carmen is strong. She always has been. But obviously, there's sorrow too. It's not easy having a child like that. So they were sad too; it would be strange if they weren't. After all, it's understandable that they would also feel some disappointment."

"And what about you?" Skarre asked. "What were your

thoughts on Tommy's future? Were you worried about it and how he would manage?"

Carmen's mother drank some more coffee. She seemed to be bothered by the questions and answered them with some reluctance.

"I'm going to tell you the truth," she said. "When Tommy was born, it was a real shock. Carmen is so young and I thought it was only older women who had children with Down syndrome. It all felt very unreal and I was devastated. So there you go, now I've said it."

"And what kind of mother was Carmen?" Skarre asked.

"The very best," Zita interjected. "They were such good parents, both of them. Tommy got all that he needed, and we helped them financially. That way Carmen could be at home, for a couple of years at least. Until Tommy went to nursery school. At Solhella, you know, there's a nursery school for children with special needs. He'd been promised a place from the age of two. The plan was that Carmen would work at the restaurant with Nicolai. They'd get by fine on two salaries. They didn't have to pay any rent for the house at Granfoss. That's to say, I am the owner and I certainly wouldn't fleece them."

"And what about Nicolai?" Skarre pressed. "Are you pleased to have him as a son-in-law?"

"Oh yes," Zita replied, without hesitation. "He's always been so good to Carmen. But he's not as strong as her, and he's completely fallen to pieces now. Carmen feels guilty because she left Tommy alone for five minutes, and she'd forgotten to close the door. Nicolai feels guilty because he was in the cellar. And I feel guilty because we didn't get the fence up in time."

"And you?" Sejer turned to Elsa. "Do you also feel guilty?"

"No," she said firmly. "I don't feel guilty. It was an accident and no one is to blame. And I don't want to hear any talk of guilt; it's bad enough as it is. Don't say things like that!"

Then she dried a tear.

"Don't you dare try," she added. "Just leave us be!"

"Certainly, we will," Sejer assured her. "It is not our intention to hound you about this. We're not out to get anyone. We just need to get a clear idea of what happened, in terms of the law."

"Of course," Elsa said and straightened her back. "I'll tell you what happened. It was very warm on August 10. Tommy was allowed to be naked for a while and was playing on his blanket. Carmen went into the bathroom and was gone for five minutes. Tommy clearly toddled down to the pond and fell off the jetty. That's what happened," she said. "And now please leave us to grieve in peace."

Zita accompanied them to the front door.

He stood for a while on the step and tried to excuse his wife.

"We understand that this is hard for you all," Sejer said, "and we certainly won't bother you with any more questions. We wish you all the best. And we hope that the youngsters will manage to pull through this without any feelings of guilt."

Zita walked a few steps down the gravel path and stood with his hands in his pockets, poking at the ground with his toe. "Yes. They'll get through it. Carmen is pretty solid. When it comes to Nicolai, he just needs a bit more time. But we'll manage."

"How did you react when Carmen got pregnant at the age of seventeen?" Sejer asked.

"We were delighted," he said swiftly. "It's such a gift, isn't it? And we thought so highly of Nicolai. We promised to do everything we could to help, and we have. We've looked after Tommy for them a lot."

He looked first at one and then the other.

"I know that you've been to the restaurant," he said suddenly. "Elisabeth called and told me that she'd had to answer some questions. I don't know what that means, the fact that you wanted to talk to her. But we assume that it's done now. We don't have anything else to tell."

He went back up the steps and then turned to them for the last time.

"I'm sure it's just your job," he said somberly. "The fact that you always think the worst. I'm trying to understand that. But you won't find anything here. It was an accident. There's nothing more to say."

Then he disappeared into the house and shut the door with a bang.

"The Women's Clinic," Sejer said to Skarre. "I've let them know that we're coming, so they'll be waiting."

16

IT WAS AFTERNOON by the time the two men arrived at Oslo University Hospital. They walked down endless corridors and through wide double doors with glass panels. And then, at the end of a corridor, a sure sign that they were in the right place: a beautiful bronze statue of a stork with a bundle in its beak. They found the staff room and one of the midwives on duty stood up and shook their hands.

"Yes," she said. "I looked after Carmen. I got your message so I waited. Please, sit down. I'll be with you in a moment."

It was a nice, homely room, with a large curved sofa and two armchairs. Flowery curtains in the windows, a large cabinet full of cups and glasses, a coffee machine, a big spacious desk. Two green filing cabinets and a PC. There was a big teddy bear in blue overalls in one corner. Above the desk, a bulletin board was full of photographs of babies in all colors and shapes and cards with messages of thanks from a number of parents. Skarre took off his jacket and went over to have a closer look at the photographs. Thank you for all your help, from Fredrikke. Thank you for looking after me at the birth, from Emilie Krantz. We wouldn't have managed without you, from Nina and Marie.

The midwife returned after a few minutes, pulled a chair out from behind the desk, and sat down. She was probably in her mid-forties, round, and dressed in a white coat over light pants and white clogs with rubber soles. She immediately inspired trust. Her hair was thick and blond and on her coat she wore a porcelain badge that said ANNE MARIE.

"Yes, I remember her," she said immediately. "It was a cesarean. She has an extremely narrow pelvis. Oh yes, I remember her, but mostly because her name, Carmen Zita, is an unusual name. Not one you forget really. And she was so young. And the child had Down syndrome. Yes, yes, I remember her well. And the father too, he was almost as young as her and incredibly shy. But I don't understand why you are here. I don't see how I can help you; has something happened?"

Sejer looked at the buxom midwife. And it struck him that she was like his wife, Elise. There was something about her hair and eyes, and the warm, assured smile that gave her dimples.

"The child is no longer alive," he told her. "Tommy drowned in a pond by his parents' house. We are investing the accident as a matter of procedure."

She was silent when she heard this, and the warm smile disappeared. She said nothing for a few long seconds, digging her hands deep into the pockets of her white coat. Then she kicked off her white clogs and sat there with bare feet that were small and narrow and golden-brown at the end of a long summer.

"Oh no, that's so sad," she said at last. "He was such a great little boy. What age did he get to?"

"Sixteen months," Sejer said. "He had just learned to walk. But tell me something. He had Down syndrome. How quickly can you see that something is wrong?"

"We see it right away," she replied. "But we have good training. And Down syndrome is not the worst thing that can happen to a child. They generally grow up into kind individuals, though they often don't live as long as other people. You could live until

86

you were ninety," she said with a brief smile. "But people who are born with the syndrome are old by the time they are fifty. If they make it to fifty, which is not always the case. As you know, their appearance is distinct and unmistakable. They are also shorter than most people, and many of them have congenital heart disease. They grow and develop slowly, both physically and mentally. Premature aging and dementia is very common, which is sad but true. And yet they can be a joy to us all. That's certainly what I think. Don't you agree?"

"How common is it for a baby to be born with Down syndrome?"

"One in every seven hundred is born with it. Which is actually quite a lot, if you think about it. On average, they live to sixty. They often have a kind of simple wisdom that we others have lost. Something genuine and honest. They are wholly themselves in everything they do and never false in any way. In fact, they make quite an impression and are rather charming. So it always warms my heart to deliver a baby like that. And I'm proud of it."

"How are they at birth?" Sejer asked. "Tell me, what signs you can see?"

"Newborns with Down syndrome are generally of normal weight and length," she said, "but they often have what we call low muscle tone. When you pick them up, they feel like a little sack of sand. They're limp. They lack the muscle tone and suppleness of other newborns. And I can tell you, it was a lot of information for the young couple to take in. We told them that they had the right to care and financial support, as well as extended leave from work.

"There's a brutal paragraph for pregnant women if they are tested before giving birth. They, of course, dream of having healthy children. Paragraph 2 of the Abortion Act says that they have the legal right to terminate the pregnancy if the fetus has Down syndrome. Which is so sad, but then, that's life."

She paused, drew breath, and put her clogs back on.

"And naturally, many parents choose to do that. They can't face the difficulties it would entail. And anything we can tell them is cold comfort. So it's a shock, no matter what, and I can understand that. No one has the right to make a moral judgment."

Sejer nodded. "Did you tell the parents right away when Tommy was born?"

"No, we waited until she had been transferred to the ward and rested a bit. It was the doctor and I who went in. It's emotionally very demanding, having to tell someone something like that," she added, "so it's good if there's two. You never get used to it."

"So you remember it well?" Skarre asked.

"Yes, I remember it well. Because of her reaction."

"What did she say? What did she do?"

The midwife let out a deep sigh. She pulled her hands out of her pockets and folded them in her lap.

"She said, 'No.'"

"What do you mean?" Skarre pressed. "Simply 'No'?"

"She was in denial. She said, 'No, you've made a mistake.' So the doctor had to tell her again that the boy had Down syndrome. That there was no room for doubt. Because that is what they often think, initially. Is it really true? Are you one hundred percent sure? And Lord only knows, it's a massive comedown. From the greatest joy to the deepest desperation. The child has finally been born after nine long months, but it's not entirely healthy. I never get used to it," she told them. "I have to steel myself before I go in. I guess you have to do that in your job as well. I mean, you must have given some people terrible news. So perhaps you know how I feel."

"Yes, we do," Sejer said in a gentle voice.

"We comforted them as best we could," she continued. "We explained her rights in terms of the future and assured them that the boy would bring them both joy and laughter. But she just kept saying no, that we had made a mistake. That time would prove that we were wrong. He would get better; he was just a bit tired. I felt for her so much, and I've had to tell people worse things in my role as a midwife. It's just part of the job."

"What about the father?" Skarre wondered. "Nicolai Brandt? How did he react?"

She thought for a moment, casting her mind back. She recalled the young man with the thin hair.

"He was incredibly quiet. Not the chatty type. But at least he understood what we were telling them, and he certainly never questioned our judgment. I felt for him too, but I remember that he did manage to muster some hope for the future. 'We should be happy for the child we've got,' he said, hugging her and the child. I can't remember if he was crying. The doctor gave them as much information as possible to instill hope. He explained that there were cases where children with Down syndrome had passed their exams, with good grades, after only three years of high school. And some had passed their driver's license test. I can't get over what you just told me, that he drowned in a pond. I don't know what your thoughts are on the matter. But let's hope that you are wrong. I mean, if you suspect the parents in any way. You're asking all these questions for a reason, and it's making me nervous. Between you and me, Carmen Zita's reaction was certainly unusual. Like she was in her own world, and it was impossible to get through. Over the years, I've had to tell many people similar things, and no one has reacted quite like her."

"How long was she in the maternity ward?"

"For five days. I remember her parents came to collect them, and her father asked to talk to the doctor, which he did. He seemed very strong and composed, and said that he would help in any way possible. I was so happy to hear that, because he seemed so dynamic."

Sejer sat in silence for a short while. He glanced up at the photographs of all the babies on the bulletin board.

"I'm assuming they never sent you a photograph," he said with a fleeting smile.

"No," she confirmed. "I never got a picture of Tommy. People send photographs because they are proud, happy, and grateful. But Carmen Zita left the ward after five days, and she was not in the slightest bit proud or grateful."

17

TWENTY-FIFTH OF AUGUST. Morning, the funeral.

Nicolai stood in the doorway and looked at her, and he didn't like what he saw. Today was the day when Tommy was to be buried. And Carmen was going to say goodbye in a wholly inappropriate dress. Short and tight with a scooped neck, it left nothing to the imagination. She normally wore it to parties, and now it just looked improper. But he also saw how beautiful she was—perfect, like a little doll. And it was clear to him why he had fallen for this girl with the white hair. No boy in the world would say no to Carmen, he thought. Not a single one. And I am no exception.

Carmen was in the bathroom and pulled herself away from her own reflection.

"You should have put something else on," she complained. "It's so embarrassing; we should have gotten a suit. People will wonder why you're not dressed up."

"Fine, but I don't have a suit," he said, feeling hurt. "You always complain, but I do as best I can. And clothes aren't important anyway. This is about Tommy."

Carmen turned back to the mirror and stared at herself. Yes, she was satisfied, Nicolai thought. Tommy was going to be buried and Carmen was satisfied with how she looked. It really bothered him. He leaned against the door frame. He knew that he wasn't good enough and was deeply ashamed of his shabby clothes. He heard a car pull into the yard and went over to the window and looked out. He waved at the people in the car and went out to meet them. Pappa Zita's sturdy frame towered over the top step; behind him was Elsa in a navy blue suit.

"How are you, my boy?" Zita asked, holding his hand. He held it for a long time, while a single tear trickled down his cheek. Then he crossed the threshold and came in. "This is a sad, sad day," he said, his eyes piercing through Nicolai. "We have to be strong."

Nicolai didn't answer. There was nothing to say, other than it was the blackest day of his life. He had not been so sad since the day his parents died in their Cessna, *Bird Dog*, in a violent storm. It all came back to him now with full force. Zita reached out his hand again but this time ruffled his hair. Nicolai did not turn away. He had always liked Zita and knew this was a clumsy caress from a man in mourning.

"Is Carmen ready?" Zita asked and walked down the hallway.

"Yes, she is," he said with a wan smile, wondering whether his parents-in-law would react to her daring dress. Just then, Carmen came out of the bathroom, tottering on high heels. The black dress was so tight that any movement was restricted to tiny steps across the floor. She gave her father a long hug, swallowed by his generous embrace and weeping bitter tears.

"Put a jacket on," her father said firmly. "Your dress is beautiful, but it's too low and not appropriate for church."

Carmen made a disappointed face and protested vociferously. It was far too warm to wear a jacket, and she didn't like her father's objections. "What kind of jacket do you mean?" Carmen whined. "The dress won't be visible otherwise."

"A cardigan," her father said. "Surely you've got a cardigan?"

"She does," said Nicolai, who had sat down on the sofa. "Your dress—it's not a party we're going to."

"I dressed up for Tommy," Carmen said, smarting. "And all you do is complain." She pouted like she always did when she didn't get her own way.

Nicolai closed his eyes and groaned. He couldn't believe that they were in this situation. They were about to go to church to bury Tommy, and this was the end. He wanted so much to be strong, to be dignified in his grief. But more than anything, he just wanted to let go and cry like a baby. Carmen turned on her heel and disappeared into the bedroom. They could hear her slamming doors and drawers. After a while she came out again with a cardigan over her arm.

"Put it on," her father said sternly. "It's a church and you need to be covered. People will react if you sit there with bare shoulders."

"If it gets too hot, I'm going to take it off," Carmen retorted. "I don't care what you say. I'm the one who's lost my baby, so I decide."

"OK. The dress is lovely," her father conceded, "but it is better suited to other occasions. Do you have anything simpler, a little more respectable?"

"No," Carmen said petulantly. "This dress fits all the rules. It's black. All my other dresses are bright and colorful. Pink and blue and yellow. And I don't want to wear pants on a day like today."

"Then you must be prepared for people to comment," he said. "You look lovely, Carmen. Don't get me wrong. I'm just trying to give you some advice. Remember that I'm older than you. There are some things I know more about."

"You're just old-fashioned; that's all it is," she said. "And what's more, you're a Catholic, and I'm not. So there."

Her father wiped the beads of sweat from his brow. Carmen's iron will overwhelmed him and made him weak.

· · ·

"I don't want to drink coffee and eat cake. I don't want to exchange clichés. I don't want to dig up old memories about what has been, the good old days," Carmen had said. She had also told the people from Sentrum and the female priest who was performing the funeral service that she couldn't face watching Tommy's coffin being lowered into the grave. The three spades of earth on the lid. So the ceremony was going to finish in the church. Nicolai had protested in his hesitant way. He felt that it would be betraying Tommy in some way not to follow him to the grave; in fact, he thought it was cowardly. But she didn't listen. It was always Carmen who won. Carmen with all the tears. Carmen whom he, in brief moments of desperation, did not believe.

Finally they were on their way in the black car, progressing slowly through the late summer streets. People were caught up with their everyday lives. Going outside to call in the kids, he thought. Shouting and taking it for granted that they would appear. Healthy and happy and full of energy. Alive and without injury. Imagine if it was all a bad dream, he thought. Was that possible? Maybe if he dozed off in the back seat, he would wake up afterward in his old, happy life. He tried to relax his body and breathed as slowly and steadily as he could. But it didn't help. He couldn't sleep and couldn't forget all the awfulness. The nights were insufferable and he couldn't bear them.

"I don't like female priests," he said. "I wish we'd gotten someone else. Sorry, but I just had to say it. You can call me what you like. But the way I feel at the moment, I don't care what you think."

Carmen turned around in the passenger seat and gave him an angry look. "Do me a favor," she said, exasperated. "She's who we're having. And she knows what she has to say. So why bring it up?"

"I don't know," he answered honestly. He felt ashamed. "I just don't like them. It should be a man, because they have more authority. I don't like female doctors either. And I don't like police-women. You'll just have to accept the fact that I think differently from you."

Elsa made no comment. It was warm, so she had taken off her suit jacket. She was wearing a white blouse with a bow at the neck underneath. Elsa had always been a bit uptight, but Nicolai had nothing against her. She was a kindly soul. When she said something, she meant it, and he liked that.

"I'm sure it will be a good funeral, all the same," Zita assured him, trying to smooth things over. They stopped for a red light. There was some roadwork and one side of the road had been closed. A convoy of eight cars drove toward them and edged past. A group of three men in safety vests filled in the holes in the road with soft, hot asphalt. An intense smell of tar lingered as they drove past.

In the church, the sun streamed in through the stained-glass windows and illuminated the images of intense red, green, and blue. A woman sowing corn; an apple tree bearing red fruit; a flock of birds departing from a branch; and a sky lit up by a bright, blazing sun. But that was not what Nicolai saw. His attention was fixed on the small coffin by the altar, drowned in a sea of blue and pink flowers. A heart, a wreath, a bouquet. He managed to walk, but his legs felt like they wanted to buckle. The church bells hurt his ears. Soon the church organ would pump out its mournful music, as though death was something beautiful. As though this would soothe the pain. Carmen walked beside him up the aisle in her short, tight dress.

She had taken her cardigan off in the car and no one could face nagging her anymore about her unsuitable outfit. Her strong will drained them all. Silent and tense, Nicolai went to the front pew on the left-hand side. He let Carmen sit down first and then took his place. Marian and Elsa followed behind. While they sat waiting for the ceremony to begin, he was assailed by a sudden panic attack. His panic made him gasp for air. Who was actually in the white coffin? Was it really Tommy, or had they made a mistake? A fateful mix-up at the last moment. Was it a baby they didn't know? He had heard about things like that, and now he broke into a cold sweat. Had everything been done correctly? Or had they been sloppy and too quick at some point? People made mistakes, just as they had with Tommy. They hadn't kept an eye on him, hadn't built a fence. The thoughts roared in his head and he could not sit still. He jumped up from the pew and went over to the coffin, looking at the two undertakers with pleading eyes.

"I want to see him," he said, determined. "I want to see my son."

Carmen was horrified. She sat there, pulling down her short dress and feeling embarrassed in front of all the people who had come. Mortified at the outburst that she could not control.

"We haven't got time for this now," she whispered from where she was sitting. "Come and sit down. People are starting to arrive, so we have to sit still." But the two people from Sentrum nodded. Finally someone was on his side. It would take quite a lot to throw them for a loop. They had been in the business for a long time, and the father had every right to see his dead child for the last time. So they stepped forward and lifted off the lid. Nicolai stood beside the coffin and held his breath. Yes, it was his Tommy, but a more pale and aged version of his son who was so full of life. Dry. Cold. Sunken. His lips were without color; the thin blond tufts of hair had been combed to one side. And he knew that under the clothes there was a seam from his neck down, because they had opened him up. Maybe his liver and kidneys were missing. Maybe he was lying there without a heart. He thought that the blue onesie was very baggy. But the sight of his son's teddy bear calmed him, lying there in the crook of his arm.

"Carmen," he called quietly. "You have to come and see."

She hesitated before standing up, as if something was holding her back. Then she reluctantly walked the few steps needed and stared down at her dead child with a pained expression.

"Yes," she said. "He's lovely. Like I always said."

Nicolai stood for a while in silence.

"Did you?" he asked in a bitter voice. "I've never heard that."

He touched the white cheek.

"He's freezing," he said to Carmen. "Feel."

18

THERE'S SOMETHING GOOD about funerals, Sejer thought
to himself afterward. Something healing, final, a sense of closure.
Even if the deceased was a child. Even if the deceased has been
killed — yes, even if the death was a catastrophe. Even Elise's funeral had felt good. Heart-rending but good. The swell of the organ and the candles, the priest's consoling voice, the liturgy. All
the flowers, the most beautiful wreaths in the world. The pews
full of mourning people, elegantly dressed, silent and pious.
Friendly hands stroking a cheek and good, warm embraces, obser-
vant eyes. Psalms, the most sublime thing he knew. *I know a castle
in heaven above.* The sun streaming in through the stained-glass
windows instilled a special peace in one's soul. But then there was
God and heaven, and that was more problematic. He glanced at
his colleague Skarre, who was sitting beside him in the Volvo.

"Good," was all he said.

"Mm," was Skarre's response. "Can you stop here by the kiosk?
My blood sugar is low. I need candy."

Sejer swung to the side and parked the car but left the engine
running. Then he sat and waited for his younger colleague. He
hadn't felt dizzy for a long time; that was a good sign. Maybe it's
passed, he thought hopefully. After all, some things do just pass.
Small everyday miracles, false alarms. A little girl on a yellow bi-

cycle rolled into the square in front of the kiosk, and he sat and watched her. She leaned her bike up against the wall and disappeared through the door, probably to buy candy. Children were insatiable when it came to candy. He wondered why. Then Skarre came out and got into the car, and they drove back onto the road. Skarre opened the bag and mumbled to himself.

"Oh damn," he said. "I meant to get jelly beans."

Sejer glanced over and saw some colorful jelly figures through the plastic.

"And is that not what you've got there?"

Skarre shook his head. "No, these are sour monsters. And that's not what I wanted. I took the wrong bag."

"But they're jelly as well?" Sejer suggested. "They certainly look like they're jelly. Is it a problem? Should I turn around?"

"No, heavens. I'll just have to live with it this once."

They drove on for a while in silence, and Skarre popped a sour jelly-bean substitute in his mouth. He smacked his lips and made a face. "Well, they're certainly sour. I've never tasted anything quite like it."

"Have you always believed in God?" Sejer asked, changing gears.

Skarre held the bag out to him, but Sejer shook his head. "Oh yes," Skarre replied. "Remember, my father was a priest. It's in my blood. What about you? Have you always been godless?"

"You make it sound like a swear word," Sejer commented. "But yes, no one in my house believed in anything at all. Sorry to be nosy, but I'm just curious. When little toddlers drown in a pond, it's hard to believe there's a meaning. That's all really. And according to your faith, everything has a meaning; isn't that right? That's what I've always struggled to understand."

He rummaged in the center console for his sunglasses. He found them and put them on, and turned on his right blinker.

Skarre took another sour monster and chewed it slowly.

"Yes, it's not easy, I have to admit. And to be honest, I sometimes falter too. But doubt is an important part of faith; that's all there is to it. And unlike you, I at least have somewhere to go with my complaints. Others flail around without focus, but I couldn't take that. I need a wailing wall."

"Fair enough," Sejer said. "You've got a point."

He stopped at a red light and they waited.

"So, you've complained to God about the loss of Tommy? Is that what you're saying?"

"Yes, I have," Skarre said. "I've had my say."

The light changed to green and Sejer drove through the intersection, the Volvo engine purring.

"And do you believe in eternal life?"

Skarre looked over at the detective inspector, and a grin spread across his face. "So, is this an interrogation?"

"Sorry," Sejer said as he turned on his left blinker. "I'm just curious. When I think of all the catastrophes, it's difficult not to ask questions. Drought, war, and lack of food. Natural disasters and disease, pain and desperation. Mothers who kill their children," he said and gave Skarre a stern look.

"Yes," Skarre replied, "they're the usual arguments. I struggle with those things too, if you want to know."

Then there was silence in the car again. After a while Skarre spoke.

"That was quite an outfit she was wearing. Carmen, I mean. I've never seen such a short dress in my life. And she could barely walk on those heels. But she's good at crying; I'll give her that. Your phone's ringing," he added. "Is your hearing getting bad?"

Sejer pulled to the side and answered, recognizing Snorrason's Icelandic accent on the other end.

"We're just on our way back from the funeral," he explained. "On our way to the station. Sorry? You've got the results?"

"Yes, I've got the results," Snorrason said. "And you're probably dealing with a murder case. The mother will have difficulties explaining this away. Is she good at explaining things?"

"Not bad," Sejer said. "We'll have to wait and see. What have you found?"

Snorrason told him, trying hard to minimize the terminology. And when he had finished, Sejer gave a quiet whistle and looked over at Skarre.

"I'll take them in for questioning then," he said brusquely. "Both of them. But we'll give them a couple of days. The boy's not long in the ground. Yes, thank you. I'll keep you posted."

He finished the call and pulled out onto the road again.

"It's as we feared," he said to Skarre. "Tommy presumably had some help in reaching heaven, or at least it certainly looks like it. You can send another complaint in to God."

19

HE WALKED SLOWLY through the empty rooms and listened. Tommy's absence was deafening. No more hiccupping laughter, no more sobbing tears. The child was dead and buried, and over time the body would decompose, disintegrate, and become dust. But the bones would remain. A fragile, tiny skeleton in the black earth.

"It's all just empty words," he said. "'Until you return to the ground, for out of it were you taken.' It's just garbage. To be honest, I feel ashamed."

Carmen wriggled out of the black dress, threw it down on the bed, and put on some everyday clothes. "The priest was nice, wasn't she?" she commented. She was now wearing jeans and a T-shirt. "Should we just take his crib down now? I mean, we don't need it anymore and it takes up quite a lot of space. We could put it in the cellar until we have another baby."

Nicolai gasped. To be saying that now—what was she thinking?

"Jesus, you're in a rush to get rid of any traces," he said, upset.

She pushed past him and went out into the kitchen. She opened a cupboard, took out a glass, and turned on the faucet. She drank water in greedy gulps until she was sated. Some water trickled down over her chin and between her breasts.

"I don't need all these reminders," she said. "It just makes things worse, going to bed at night with the empty crib staring at us. That's just the way I am; I want to forget it. I don't want to be upset by memories."

He walked into the living room and sat down on the sofa. He felt so tired, like he'd shifted down a gear. Everything that normally happened in his body was now so slow, and he felt cold, despite the late summer heat. The warmth of the sun pressed in against the windows and glittered on the surface of the vile pond with its single water lily.

"Maybe we should move," Carmen called from the kitchen. "Get away from it all. Start again somewhere else. I can talk to Dad. Because if I want a new house, he'll get me a new house."

Nicolai protested. He felt they had to stay in the neighborhood, close to the church and the boy. Tommy should be within easy reach, and the grave by Møller Church was only twenty minutes away. He was up between the birch trees beside Louisa.

Carmen had come into the living room. She stood there with the glass of water in her hand. He saw her nipples stiffen under her T-shirt, despite the heat. He had never seen a girl with such small breasts as Carmen; she could almost be a boy.

"If we dismantle the crib, it will take less room," she said. "And there's so much junk in the cellar already."

Junk, Nicolai thought. So she thinks Tommy's bed is junk.

Carmen drank some more water and dried her mouth.

"I want to start working again," she said with determination. "The days go faster. Don't you want to start working again too?"

He nodded. She went into the kitchen again and he heard her opening a drawer.

"Do you think they've buried him by now?" she shouted. "Was it stupid of us not to go to the grave?"

"Yes, it was stupid. I told you it was. You could have listened.

You always want your own way, but I've got opinions too. Opinions and wishes."

"We can go there tomorrow, if you like," she called, in an attempt to placate him. "To look at the grave. It's great, isn't it, that he got a place under the birch trees? Just like I wanted. I'm so glad."

Tommy is dead and buried, he thought, and you stand here and say you're glad. Jesus, you're unbelievable. But everyone grieves differently, he reminded himself. Carmen is not someone to dwell on things. She's impatient and wants to move on. I have to remember that, he thought. But he felt overwhelmed by her energy and will all the same.

"I'm sure we'll have another baby, sooner or later," she said. "Life goes on, doesn't it? You do agree?"

He went into the kitchen and sat down at the table. He studied her narrow back at the counter.

"But that's not what I want," he said defiantly. "Not anymore, at least. Don't go on about it; it just makes me depressed."

"Well, I'm sorry," she said, offended. "I'm just trying to hold things together. It's hard for me too, you know."

He looked at her with doleful eyes. I don't think I love her anymore, he thought. He felt exhausted and helpless and sad. Everything we had is falling to pieces and too much has happened to get over it. How, he thought, will it ever pass?

"We need to eat," Carmen said after a few seconds' silence. "I'll make some spaghetti and meatballs."

He declined. No, he was sure he didn't want any food. He wanted to punish himself by not eating to atone for Tommy's death, for the fact that he hadn't looked after him better and put up that damn fence. Instead he had gone down into the cellar to tinker with bikes. As if that was important. There are always moments like that, he thought. A few minutes when the child is not being watched. But then Tommy had just learned to walk, and the door was open and he had toddled off toward the glittering water. Children and water. Of course it was just waiting to happen. He followed Carmen with his eyes as she wiped the counter with a cloth. She opened a cupboard and took out a box of spaghetti.

"Whatever the priest says," he started, "Tommy won't go to heaven. We're both hypocrites. We're hypocrites because we got a priest, and I feel like shit."

She turned around and looked at him in exasperation. "Speak for yourself. Others can believe what they like. I can't imagine where else the soul would go. And Tommy had a soul. You agree on that, don't you?"

Yes, he thought, that's true. But it was extinguished with his body. No living body, no energy, and therefore no soul.

"So you think you're going to meet Tommy again?" he sneered. "Up in heaven?"

"Don't be so mean," she said. "It's just that I believe in another existence. If you want to play the atheist, that's fine by me. But you don't have the answer either. And there are smarter people than you who believe, so there."

He leaned his elbows on the table and had to admit that she had a point. He watched as she worked at the counter. She was quick, Carmen, everything was fast. And he was actually very hungry. He couldn't ignore the fact that he needed food.

"Did you see what I got from Pappa Zita?" she asked. "I got a present."

Yes, he had, but had forgotten it in the midst of everything else. Pappa Zita had given her a package when they got back to the car after the church service was over. He guessed it was a book; it was certainly a slim, flat package. Perhaps a book about death that she could read and find comfort in. That would be so like Zita, because that was the way he thought—that everything could be said in words.

"I'm going to keep a diary," she said contentedly. "He wants me to write about what's happened. And about everything that's going to happen in the future. But you're not allowed to read it. Diaries are secret, so there."

She opened one of the kitchen drawers and held up the book. It was beautiful and small, with a red cover. There was a label on the front where she had written her name in careful letters.

"Can I have a look?" he asked, holding his hand out. He opened it at the first page, which was still blank.

"Are you going to write in it every day?"

"Yes," she said, determined. "I'm going to write every single day."

"But what if nothing happens?"

"Of course something will," she said. "Things happen all the time. Today we buried Tommy. Tomorrow we'll go and visit his grave under the birch trees. And the day after, we'll go to the stonemasons out by Kruttverket. We did agree to do that, didn't we? And if nothing happens, then I can write just that," she said, full of enthusiasm. "Today is over and nothing has happened."

She went over to the desk and put the book away in the bottom drawer. "Hands off," she said with a smile. Then she went back into the kitchen and put the spaghetti in the boiling water, leaving the lid off to one side. She sat down at the table and took his hands in hers and squeezed them hard.

"It'll get easier," she said without doubt. "Even the most painful things pass. But you can't think of the future."

"No," he objected. "It will never get easier."

"You don't want to forget," she said quietly.

"No, that's right. And I can see that you do. I don't understand how you're made."

"I've always been strong," she said. "You know that I'm really like Dad."

20

Morning.

The late summer heat continued, and many people were now longing for autumn with its soothing dusk, cool nights, and calming dark. But from daybreak the sun burned relentlessly in a blue sky. It stung one's eyes and parched the fields. Nature was thirsty and needed some fresh, regenerating rain.

It wasn't that he was triumphant, that wasn't his nature. Revenge, hate, and bitterness had never been part of his life and had never played a role in his very particular profession. To prove guilt or innocence, to clear or condemn — that was his duty. He was not looking forward to the interview; it was probably a match he would not win in the end. There were only losers in this case: Tommy, Nicolai and Carmen, Marian and Elsa. And yet he felt reinvigorated. His intuition had always been strong, and he had the feeling he would be proved right, that the boy's life had been snuffed out intentionally.

Carmen came into the room and he showed her to a seat. They weren't in the office this time, with its lovely view from the window and his dog on a blanket. Now they were in one of the station interview rooms, the saddest room there was. Bare with coarse stone walls and glaring lights. She remained standing for a moment and looked around the Spartan room. She seemed confused and uncertain but tried to compose herself. It was not a particularly welcoming room and reminded her more of a cave in the mountains. No windows and nothing on the walls. Just the uncomfortable lighting, two chairs and a table, a laptop, a work lamp with a halogen bulb, and strip lights.

"I don't understand what all the fuss is about," she said. "I've got nothing more to say; you've got to stop."

"We'll see," Sejer said phlegmatically. "Sit yourself down, because we need to talk. It's important."

She was wearing a sleeveless dress that was almost as short as a T-shirt. When she sat down, it slid up over her thighs, revealing how thin she was. She couldn't weigh much more than ninety pounds, give or take a couple. The sandals on her feet had obviously given her blisters, as there were bandages on her heels.

He sorted his papers, pressed the record button on the Dictaphone, and put it down on the table between them. It was about the size of a cigarette pack, with an ominous blinking red eye.

"Carmen," he said gravely. "I would like to go through what happened by Damtjern on August 10 once more. It's true that you have already given a statement, but we have found some striking new evidence that means that we need to go through this again."

"What have you found?" she asked, playing tough.

Thus far, she was not giving an inch.

"We've done an autopsy on Tommy," Sejer reminded her. "This involved a thorough internal and external examination. A number of samples were taken. Of his blood, his saliva, and his tissue. The pathologist doesn't miss much, and you of course have the right to know what we have found. Naturally we look for signs of external violence, among other things. And for poison or what we call 'toxins.' The lab results have come in and that is why you have been called in again. This is serious, Carmen. Do you understand what I am saying?"

Carmen Zita pulled herself together. Poison and external violence, mere fantasy, she thought. She raised her chin and was defiant and proud and unassailable.

"And no," he said, before she had time to protest. "We have found no evidence of violence. Nor have we found toxins. But we did find something else."

She nodded, almost mechanically. Her lips were tight and he knew her heart was beating faster, because her cheeks flushed red with the sudden surge.

"So, Carmen," he said firmly, "think back and be as precise as you can. The tenth of August, around one o'clock. Nicolai is in the cellar working on a bike. You're busy in the kitchen. Tommy is playing around on the floor without any clothes on, because it's so warm."

"Yes," she complied. "I was preparing some food. And when I'd finished, I had to go into the bathroom. And I'm really sorry, but I was gone for quite a while. But that's hardly a crime, is it?"

"Why?" Sejer asked. "Tell me what it was that kept you there. I'm curious."

"I'd put some socks in to soak, so I rinsed them and hung them up to dry. I don't wash socks in the machine because they shrink. And it took a few minutes. So there, now you know."

"Can you be more precise than a few?" Sejer asked.

"Well, I don't know. Maybe six or seven minutes. Or more, I'm not sure. When I came back into the kitchen, Tommy was gone. So I went to look for him in the living room, in the hallway, and in the bedroom. It took some time before I realized that he wasn't in the house. I didn't think about the pond, not right away. But then it's always been there, and I didn't think he'd be able to walk that far in such a short time. And he had no shoes on and the gravel is sharp."

Again her hand went up to her eyes, and the tears started to flow steadily.

"So I ran out and down to the pond and I saw him right away. Beside the jetty. It wasn't my fault, no matter what you think."

Sejer made a brief note.

"What do you think I think?" he commented patiently.

"Well," she said hesitantly, "that it was my fault. But I don't have eyes in the back of my head and I'm totally innocent."

"So what did you do then? Tell me."

"I threw myself into the water as fast as I could. I pulled him up onto the grass and tried to give him mouth-to-mouth. But it didn't help—nothing helped. He was gone. And there was all this foam around his mouth. I was terrified."

"How long did you try for?" he asked.

"Oh, I can't remember. I screamed for Nicolai to come. He panicked as well and was down by the pond a few seconds later. And he tried to revive him too, and I was so sure that he'd manage, because Nicolai is so good at all kinds of things. But no matter what he did, he couldn't get Tommy's heart started. When the paramedics came, they took over. They're obviously much better at it than us, but they didn't manage either, even though they seemed to try forever. When they said there was no point in continuing, I just about fainted. They gave up right in front of my eyes. It's over, they said, and one of the men was crying like a baby. We were both crying and Nicolai was in shock."

At this point in her account, she changed position in her chair, as if she wanted to emphasize what she was saying.

"And I couldn't understand why the police said we had to go down to the station. It was an accident," she said conclusively.

She had said all she wanted to say. Sejer jotted something down, the thoughts racing through his mind, a combination of sorrow and sympathy. He felt no joy in breaking down her story. After all, she was practically a child herself, and he was a sympathetic person. But there were still so many questions to be answered.

He was always fascinated by this moment, the moment when the mask fell away. Thanks to a combination of science, intuition, and sense.

"Carmen," he said calmly, "why are you lying?"

"But I'm not lying!" she cried. "Leave me alone; I can't take being blamed anymore. I did what I could, but it was too late!"

Sejer let her sit in silence for a while, her outburst vibrating in the air. Meanwhile he prepared his next move.

"Carmen," he said quietly. "It didn't happen the way you've told me. You have the opportunity now to tell the truth. I'm still waiting for the only possible explanation. Tommy has been examined by a pathologist and a number of tests were done. The cause of death was drowning; we have established that. But he didn't drown in the pond. And that is no unfounded claim. It is a documented fact."

"What?" she said uncertainly. "What do you mean? I don't understand what you're going on about. I've told you what happened!"

She stared wide-eyed at the Dictaphone that lay between them on the table. The red eye was still blinking, documenting her every breath.

"Don't say things like that; it makes me nervous," she added.

"Tommy had water in his lungs," Sejer said. "But not the water from Damtjern. The water in Tommy's lungs contained soap."

There. He'd said it. He made a brief note and then looked at her across the table.

"So how do you explain that? Why are you lying?"

The silence that followed was so absolute you could hear the traffic on the street outside, despite the room being sound insulated. So, not the muddy water from Damtjern, but soapy water. That could not be explained away. Everything seemed to stop. He could see that she was searching for words but could not find them.

"What actually happened, Carmen? Did he drown in the bath-tub? Because you know, you won't get away with this now that we've found the evidence. I want the truth about what happened, my dear, even if we have to sit here until Christmas."

"Am I suspected of something?" she asked lamely. "You might as well tell me like it is. If I'm suspected of something, then I've got the right to a lawyer. I'm not going to answer any more stu-pid questions!" she said, bursting out with a sob. Her tears were streaming steadily and evenly. A deep red flushed her cheeks.

"Of course you'll get a lawyer. But the fact is that you've given a false statement. And that is serious. That is where you stand at the moment. But you have a chance now to tell the truth once and for all. Tell me what actually happened. I'm sitting here, listening."

Carmen Zita continued to weep bitter tears at the injustice. "OK, I'll tell you, but you have to believe me then," she pleaded. "You see, I found him in the bathtub. And it was already too late."

She leaned back in the chair, crossed her arms, and stared at him in anticipation. Sejer listened and made notes. Found in the bathtub, OK, that was possible. The incident might still be an ac-cident. In which case she could perhaps be tried for negligence, and she was presumably aware of this.

"So, you'd put him in a bath of warm, soapy water. Do you use the big bathtub, or do you have a special baby one?"

"Yes," she said, "he was in the big bathtub. And it was pretty full. I had to support his back so he wouldn't slide under. I was on my knees on the floor. We were playing with some rubber ducks; he loved that kind of thing."

"Why did you leave him?"

She shook her fair head. "I didn't, I didn't leave him. I'm not stupid, you know. No one would leave such a small baby in a bath-tub full of water and I'm not totally irresponsible." She leaned forward over the table and looked at him with earnest eyes. "I had a fit," she said dramatically. "It happens every now and then."

"A fit? What kind of fit? Explain."

Again he heard the hum of the traffic from the street outside. But then the world disappeared again and he was absolutely focused on the present, there in the room.

"I've got a serious brain disorder," she confessed. She pouted and pushed her lower lip forward, as if she was sulking.

"What do you mean by disorder?" he asked.

"I've got epilepsy," she explained. "I was washing him when I had a major seizure. I was flat out on the floor for quite a while. When it was over, he was lying at the bottom of the bathtub and it was too late. He had swallowed loads of water and I just panicked. I didn't really know what I was doing. Surely you can understand that," she added. "I was so scared, I just went to pieces."

Hmm, he thought, a seizure. Cramps and loss of consciousness. He checked that the Dictaphone was still recording. All Carmen's words would be stored in the little box and could be used for or against her in court on the final day.

"I thought I might be charged with negligence if I told the truth," she continued. "So I carried him down to the pond. Then I could say that he'd gone there by himself, on his own two feet. Right to the end of the jetty and over the edge. It would be a more believable explanation in a way, and it wouldn't really be my fault. Just an unfortunate accident. That's what I thought. It probably sounds stupid, but I wasn't myself. You've got to believe me; it was a major fit. So I carried him out to the pond and let him sink. I pretended that was what happened, made up a new story. Then I went to get Nicolai. And I don't want you bothering him anymore, because it's definitely not his fault!"

There was silence again following this outburst. He waited. He could not help but wonder at this new turn of events. For all he

114

knew, she might be telling him the truth now. A very intricate story but perhaps too fantastic to be a lie.

"How long have you had epilepsy?"

"I was born with it," she said. "I've always had it, and it's pretty bad."

"Do you take medicine?"

"Yes," she replied. "Of course I take medicine; don't be ridiculous! I don't have fits that often, but when I do they're big ones and they last a long time. Maybe once a month. We didn't get enough air when we were born, you see. I'm actually a twin and it was a difficult birth. My sister Louisa died right away; she was only alive for an hour. And she only weighed three pounds. I weighed six, so you can imagine. I was the stronger of the two of us, and I'm proud of it. So there."

"And how do you feel after a blackout like that?" he inquired.

"Not good," she said quickly. "Dizzy, confused, and weak. I don't really know what I'm doing. I'm just not with it for quite a long time. And later I can't remember those first few minutes; it's like they've been erased. More often than not I have to lie down, and I usually sleep for a few hours. But I've lived with epilepsy all my life, so I'm used to it. And Nicolai is too, and Dad of course. He knows how it is and he understands me."

Sejer pondered what she had told him. It was absolutely plausible. She might get away with this version; stranger things had happened in Norwegian courts. A good lawyer. A charming defendant. A constant stream of tears and a serious, chronic condition that gave her fits.

"I shouldn't have given him a bath without Nicolai's help," she said and sniffed. "But he was so busy with his old bikes. All I had to do was shout if I could feel a fit coming on. But I didn't this time."

"So normally you can feel it beforehand? That you're about to have a fit?"

"Sometimes I get a little warning. But I didn't this time. It hit me before I had time to think, and I just collapsed on the floor. And Tommy slipped out of my arms and went under. You have to believe me, because it's true!"

"Carmen," Sejer said calmly, "what you have just told me is very serious indeed. You tried to hide the truth, which is not good. You should have told us this right away. I've given you more than one chance. I'm afraid this may be taken to court and you will have to stand witness. There's no getting away from it now. If you had told us from the start—well, it would have been better, but lying in your statement only encourages suspicion. Do you understand what I'm saying?"

"But I've told you the truth now," she sobbed. "Will I have to go to prison?"

"That's for the judge to decide. We may have to remand you in custody, but let's cross that bridge when we get to it. That's up to the prosecution and defense. But you will, as you said earlier, need to get a good lawyer. Now, have you told me the truth about what happened? Be honest."

"Yes," she cried. "It's the truth. I got cramps and fell on the floor. Tommy must have gone under and swallowed loads of water and got it in his lungs. It was an accident! I was stupid, but I'm not guilty of anything else no matter what you think. So just leave it now!"

"Who is your physician?" Sejer asked.

"Dr. Morris," she said, taken aback. "At the medical center on Ågårds Plass. Why do you need to know?"

"I want to see your medical history, all the details," he said somberly. "It might just save you."

21

Now, for the very first time, my dear friend, my new confidant,
I'm going to write in my book with a red cover. I'm going to write
down everything that's happened, once and for all. I'll try to be
honest, but it might take some time, because the truth is buried
deep inside. That's not just true of me, but of everybody. So this
is the situation: at least I don't have to go to prison, because the
case is still not clear in terms of the prosecution. That's what he
said, the scary inspector, and I was so relieved. I'm young and I
don't have a criminal record, and I've got a good lawyer. My lawyer's name is Fredrik Friis, and he's as old as Dad. It's such a relief that he's on my side. No matter what, he'll support me. He's
says that everything will be fine, that the court will have to believe that it was because of the seizure and that my confusion afterward had terrible consequences. That's the words he used, and
I'm using them too, because they're such a comfort. He will be the
one talking in court and people will listen to him. Nicolai is going in for questioning this afternoon, but he's got nothing more
to tell. Just that I shouted in a panic when I saw the catastrophe.
It was too late by the time he got there. I feel sorry for Nicolai.
He's taken this really badly. His life has just fallen to pieces, like
there's no way back. God, I was so scared when the police said

they'd found evidence. I had no idea that they could find out all those details just by doing some tests. Gives me the shivers. All the things you haven't thought about, water with soap in it, something as awful as that. But Dad is my greatest comfort. He believes me and will help in any way he can. He's my rock. And now he's heard my new statement. Nicolai got really angry, shouted and screamed—that you could do something like that, are you crazy? was what he said. He was raging and he doesn't do that very often. I'll say that for him. And then I started to cry, and he withdrew into himself as he always does when I cry. He sat there and clammed up and it was impossible to get through to him. And he knows what I'm like after a big fit. Yes, I would say that I've got a strong case.

I wish I'd had brothers or sisters.

I often think about it, and every time I do, I get really upset. A brother or a little sister. Someone to lean on when I feel upset, someone to complain to when things go wrong. Someone to confide in. It would have been so nice. But now I have you, dear diary, and you will also do the trick. But it's sad that Louisa died. Because otherwise it would have been the two of us. Maybe it's my fault. Maybe I was too greedy. I took all the food. So I've been punished for it and now I'm alone. And what about Nicolai, poor thing, who has no family whatsoever. It's not surprising he's so attached to Pappa Zita, and I'm so glad he is. Because everyone needs somewhere to go when life gets stormy. When life is unbearable. But I will do my best. Diaries exist for the truth to be told, and I will do what I can. There's always the fear that someone else might read it, even though Nicolai definitely won't sneak a look because he's got such high morals. He's quiet, he's proper, he's polite. That's why I chose him. In the evenings he sits at the computer surfing the Internet, checking Facebook. Maybe he's got friends there that I don't know about. It's possible, boys, maybe even girls. I never bother him. I just let him get on with it. I'm really fond of Nicolai. But I don't think I'm in love with him, that's gone forever. He's become a habit. But a habit I like a lot, to be fair. It's got a lot to do with Tommy, but so much is broken now. Maybe we'll just become another statistic about relationships breaking up. Apparently it's not that unusual, I've read about such things. How can we move on, I wonder, when it was Tommy who held us together? And now, after, it's so incredibly empty, so deafeningly quiet in all the rooms. But the quiet is quite nice, to be honest. No one crying, no one making a fuss. It's just a relief. I'm keeping a close eye on Nicolai and how he's feeling. In case he breaks down, because I think he might. He's so fragile, like he's falling apart at the seams. And now it's just him and me, suddenly like strangers, rattling around like two stones in a tin.

22

"CARMEN'S NOT EASY," Nicolai said. "She's so stubborn and willful and obstinate. She decides everything and she does it with such energy. Maybe it's just that I'm weak; I don't dare assert myself. I just do everything she says, and it's been like that for years. It's like she's an expert in every field, and I just don't make the mark."

"She has epilepsy," Sejer said. "How do you feel about that?"

"I feel sorry for her, because it's not particularly nice," he said. "It's horrible and it leaves her confused. To be honest, that's true for me too. Normally she wants to keep quiet about it, as if it's something to be ashamed of. But that's not true. She's always had it, but she doesn't have fits that often. She takes Rivotril. I'd guess she has a seizure about once a month. But they're pretty major, the fits. She's out cold for quite a while, and it's pretty dramatic to see it as well. The cramps are powerful and last for a long time. I haven't told Carmen, but I've never gotten used to it. It really freaks me out. She's so confused and outside herself afterward. Whereas I'm worn out with fright and worry."

"What do you mean by outside herself?" Sejer asked. "Do you mean that she behaves irrationally?"

"Yes, totally, she just wanders all over the place. I have to shepherd her like a sheep dog until it's passed. And you know, it's quite some time. It's like a blackout."

"So after a fit she can be a bit muddled? As she explained to me when she was interviewed?"

"Yes, that's right; she gets muddled. It's like she has to start all over again. She doesn't know what day it is, that sort of thing. She does stupid things that she forgets about afterward. It's quite frightening really."

"Do you have any thoughts about her new statement?"

"Of course I do. When I heard, I couldn't believe it. I mean, really. She could have called for me; I wasn't far away. But I guess she panicked, and I'm trying very hard to understand."

"Let me ask you something about her epilepsy," Sejer said gravely. "Can she tell beforehand if she's about to have a fit?"

"Yes, she can. Not always, but mostly, yes."

"And what does she do then?"

"She lies down flat on the sofa or the floor. That is, she does what she can before it starts and she's pretty careful. I feel really ashamed, but I don't care as much about Carmen anymore as I should," he added, with a new frankness.

Sejer gave him a paternal look. "I see," he said. "And how much do you think you should care about her? Life is not easy and you're not duty-bound to love anyone this much or that much. So be kind to yourself."

"What about you?" Nicolai inquired. "Do you love your wife as much as you did before?"

"My wife?" he said. "What can I say? She died many years ago. She was only forty, so I live alone now. Well, with Frank, that is, the dog you met the last time. I don't have a bad word to say about Frank, but it's not the same as having a partner."

"Oh, I'm sorry. I didn't know."

Sejer's smile was melancholy. "No, how could you know? But perhaps it's true to say I never had the time to get bored. My feelings are just as strong now; I guess they will never fade. Though sometimes I wish they would. So I could move on. I might have found myself a new wife. But whenever I meet someone new, I get cold feet and it feels like being unfaithful. We got married in church, as if that explains anything. So there you go. Now we've both confessed," he said, smiling. "Tell me how Tommy came between you."

"Well, we didn't really agree on how to bring him up. Carmen said I spoiled him; she was much stricter than I was. She wouldn't pick him up when he was lying in bed crying, that sort of thing. And I've asked myself what it would have been like had he been normal. You know, if everything would have been better then. But Tommy was the best and I was really proud of him. I had a son and I was going to teach him to repair bikes. And to play football, for that matter. If he was physically fit enough to run after a ball, that is. But Carmen was disappointed. She never said it straight out, but I saw it in so many little ways, that she resented it."

"Give me an example," Sejer said.

"Well," Nicolai started, "one time she was at work in the café. She'd taken a couple of extra shifts because of illness. And I turned up unannounced with Tommy in the carriage. I just dropped in to say hello, because I thought she'd be happy to see us. But I was wrong. I walked all the way from Granfoss, and it was a lovely walk. But she wasn't happy to see us at all when we came through the door. The other two, Siri and Elisabeth, cooed around the carriage. She didn't normally like showing him off to others but she made an effort and played all happy and proud. But I know Carmen; I could tell she was just pretending."

He fell silent and looked at Sejer with troubled eyes.

"And that's how she is all the time," he concluded. "She's just pretending."

23

AFTERWARD NICOLAI DROVE back home to Granfoss in the blue Golf. He found Carmen in the kitchen. She was cutting up some meat; her movements were fast and efficient and the knife was sharp. She was wearing a denim miniskirt and a pink T-shirt with writing across the front: I HAVE THE PUSSY, SO I'M IN CHARGE.

She turned and looked at him, standing expectantly with the knife in her hand.

"Well, what did you talk about?" she asked. "What did he ask you? My God, they don't quit."

"Whatever," Nicolai said and shrugged. "I can't be bothered to tell you everything. We talked about a few things and I actually quite like him. He's decent and fair."

"But what did he ask you? Come on, tell me. We're both part of this; the least I can expect is for you to be open."

"Open? You're telling me to be open?"

That would give her something to think about, he mused. He didn't need to tell her anything. So she gave up and started talking manically about something else.

"I had a thought," she said. "Shall we plant some ivy on Tommy's grave? It looks after itself and it doesn't wither like other plants, so it's always lush and green."

She turned back to the meat and put the first pieces in the pan. It started to sizzle and seconds later he could smell it.

Nicolai thought about her suggestion. He tried to imagine the gravestone covered in leaves. He kicked off his shoes and sat down in a chair. Looking up at her expectant face, he suddenly had an irrepressible urge to be difficult. Because he was hurting. And because he didn't understand how she could behave as if nothing had happened. She was standing there cutting up meat like before, with quick, efficient, and determined movements.

"No," he said firmly. "Not ivy. It takes over everything. The name and everything will disappear," he objected. "It grows like a weed. Ivy is better for old people."

She sighed and looked slightly irritated. "You never agree with anything, do you?" she snapped. "You're just a grump. Ivy is beautiful, with red and green leaves. It's like a fairy tale. Did you know it's got loads of tiny suckers? That's why it climbs everything, over glass and stone and trees. I really can't see why you'd say no, because ivy is beautiful."

He swallowed his exasperation, stood up again, and went over to the kitchen cupboard. He took out plates and glasses and put them on the table. Then he got out the cutlery and napkins and filled a jug of water. He stole secret glances at her slim back over by the stove.

"What do you reckon the police are thinking after your new statement?" he asked. "What if they don't believe you?"

She turned around again and looked straight at him. "They haven't decided whether to prosecute yet or not," she said. "That's what he said, the inspector, and he knows about things like that. And I wasn't remanded in custody. It was an accident and you know how muddled I can be after a major fit. So don't go on about it. I don't want to hear any more, OK?"

She brushed her hair back from her eyes, put some more meat in the pan, and started to chop the onion. Her eyes immediately started to sting and smart.

"No matter what you think, I loved Tommy just as much as you," she said after a pause. "Don't go thinking you had something special; I was his mother. And I can't help the fact that I'm stronger than you. You know that I get it from Dad, so you just have to deal with it. You can wallow as much as you like, but I want to move on. We have to. I know that you need me to carry the load, and that's fine. But I get tired too sometimes, so there."

He started to feel guilty. Yes, she did have to carry the load, because he was barely capable of a clear thought. And the guilt engulfed him with great force. That he hadn't taken more responsibility. That he had fled the heat of the kitchen and escaped to the cool cellar. Away from the heat and Carmen and the child, down to the peace and quiet. Was that really what he wanted, to get away? From the responsibility and obligations? He took the salt and pepper from the spice rack and put them on the table. Her words cut him to the quick. Because he did have something special with Tommy. A devotion that was now lost forever. It wouldn't have been like that with any other kid, he was sure of it. He couldn't even imagine another situation like that.

"Before," he started, and had to clear his throat. "Before Tommy was born and it was just the two of us, we used to have lots of parties. The house was full of people and music and laughter. Then suddenly you didn't want people to come here anymore. You didn't want people to see him. You might as well tell the truth, because I know anyway."

Carmen dropped the knife and looked at him. "Stop talking like that! You have no idea what it's like when people stare; I couldn't stand it! Having to explain the whole time and answer questions. Can he do this and can he do that and what about the future—so

126

just stop it! Things are bad enough as they are, and you're making them worse."

She collapsed into a chair by the kitchen table and hid her face in her hands. He couldn't bring himself to comfort her, so he went over to the stove and took the pan off the burner.

"You didn't like it either," she said and dried her tears. "You didn't really like the fact he was the way he was. You just didn't want to admit it. Whatever you think, you're no better than me."

She got up again and added the chopped onion to the pan.

She turned around and looked him straight in the eye one last time. "You've been behaving like you're the only victim the whole time," she snapped. "So may I remind you that there are two of us. I've lost my little boy as well and I'll never get over it. You can sit down now," she added. "Supper is almost ready. That's if you're going to allow yourself to have food at all."

24

AFTER QUESTIONING NICOLAI, Sejer walked along the promenade by the river in the low afternoon sun. His dog was busy looking for some sort of trophy as usual, something he could present to his master. Often it was a stick, but sometimes it was an empty cigarette pack or a banana skin—the sort of thing that people drop as they wander nonchalantly through the town. He would carry the small treasure in his mouth for the rest of the walk, trotting through the streets with his head held high, so very proud. He would carry his precious find all the way back to the apartment, where he would immediately set about to ripping it to shreds.

The river flowed heavy and silently. Sejer stared at the swirling currents and felt soothed by the running water. He always did because water put out the fire that burned in his heart. A couple of swans watched him from the bank with their black beady eyes but soon lost interest and swam out onto the water. Frank had already found his trophy for the day. It was a yellow pacifier, and he looked pretty comical with it in his mouth. It would come home with them, where he would break it up into its separate components: the rubber, the plastic ring, the cover. Sejer felt dizzy. Not alarmingly so. Just a hint, a reminder of the situation. I'm a slow-poke, he thought. Must be my age. As he walked, he admired the boats moored in a row along the river, from modest wooden boats to more luxurious cruisers. When he got to Skutebrygga, he spotted an empty table and sat down by the water. He decided to treat himself to a beer in the sun, to enjoy the last remnants of summer. The fountain in the river that normally spouted out water in high elegant arcs had been dismantled, and he realized he missed it. He felt lightheaded again and forced himself to sit still in the chair. The dizziness came and went but was getting stronger now. The thought of falling to the floor in a café in the middle of town did not appeal to him. He picked up his beer and drank in careful sips. He thought about Carmen and her latest statement. It was so remarkable that it could well be true, because, after all, reality was complex and anything was possible. He also worried about Tommy as he sat there with his ice-cold beer—that he might never find out the truth.

25

DEAR DIARY,

What people don't know won't hurt them. I live by that simple rule, because I think it's true and pretty well said, don't you think? And right now up at Granfoss it's still warm. What a long, hot summer! All the flowers around the house have died. I haven't had the energy to keep them alive. There's no tap outside and it's so heavy carrying the water out. There are dry yellow patches on the lawn and it doesn't look particularly nice. We need rain by the cloud-load for things to grow. And no, I don't feel I'm to blame. But Nicolai is so full of accusations, and to tell the truth, he's losing it. Every day when I come into the living room in the morning, I see his whiskey glass on the table. And it doesn't bother him that I see. He's not ashamed. If this is a war, then I'll win. Because unlike Nicolai, I'm a survivor, and I'm proud of that.

26

PAPPA ZITA WAS a kind and generous man and he really loved
the two youngsters. He felt that they were under his wing and
that he was responsible for them. And now he wanted to give
them a vacation. It was of course well meant, but a trip to the
Mediterranean to help them forget was not something Nicolai believed would work. He couldn't run away from his grief; the idea
was impossible.

"Well, take your grief with you, then," Carmen said, exasperated, "if you need to have it close by at all times. I don't understand you. Surely forgetting is a good thing."

He didn't answer. Yes, the grief would follow them. The loss
of Tommy was like a constant scream in his befuddled brain.
He tried to be kind and cooperative—arguing just made things
worse—and there had been enough tears and suffering now,
surely. They had to get on with their lives, despite all that had
happened. He was painfully aware of this, but deep in his heart,
he didn't want to go on. Only when his grief was at its most intense was he close to Tommy; if he opened his life to joy again, his
boy would slip from his arms and disappear. The thought of living the rest of his life without Tommy left him weak and breath-
less. He spent a lot of time in the cellar. He liked being down there
in the semi-dark with the broken bicycles. It was cool and pleas-

ant, and he didn't like the heat. It only made him tired and list-less. He never had enough energy, whereas it was so much easier for Carmen. Everything was easier for her. And that was exactly what he had fallen for once upon a time—that she was always upbeat and always found a solution. She could cry like a baby one minute, and then suddenly be happy and forget her woes the next. He had fallen for her ability to survive. He had seen it as a great strength, something that impressed him both in body and soul. Now it bothered him that she was taking Tommy's death so lightly. That she wanted to move so quickly, that she wanted to forget: the crib in the cellar, the clothes out of the drawers into garbage bags and all the way to the thrift shop. Other unknown children would play in Tommy's clothes, laugh and cry in his one-sies, sleep on his pillow, under his comforter. He couldn't bear the thought of it. One day he noticed to his horror that the beautiful photograph of their boy had been taken down from its place above the sofa. He stopped in his tracks and put his face in his hands. He couldn't believe what he was seeing; he was dismayed.

"There's no need to get so wound up," Carmen said. "I've just moved it. It's hanging in the bedroom now, above our bed. Isn't that better? Now we can look up at his smiling face before we go to sleep. Get over it; I meant well."

He tried to calm himself down. But his pulse was racing and his cheeks were flushed. He wanted so badly to be patient. He really wanted them to agree, but she was too fast. She thought and acted on impulse, while he sat and wallowed and watched her actions with alarm. She managed to hurt him all the time. She raised her voice and called him a whiner, and he couldn't stand it. When she said that, he felt desperate and lost any hope. It was so mean, so heartless. No, he couldn't take it anymore. He didn't often cry, but sometimes when they argued, he made straight for the cellar to stand over an old bicycle and weep.

"Well, if you don't want to go, I'll go on my own," Carmen said firmly. "And then while you sit down by the pond wallowing, I'll be lying on the beach. What should I say to Pappa Zita? Any suggestions?"

"No," he said hesitantly, taking his time. "It would be betraying Tommy somehow. Long days in the warm sun, when he's lying there alone in the graveyard."

"Mom will look after his grave," she said. "Every day. And by the way, I forgot to tell you that she's planted some ivy."

27

TWENTY-FIRST OF SEPTEMBER. Morning at Oslo Airport.

"So," Nicolai said as he picked at a slice of pizza, "I called the airport to ask what kind of plane we were flying on. Because it's interesting to know. There's a big difference between the different types of airplanes. And we're going to be on a huge Airbus."

"What are you worrying about now?" Carmen sighed. "You're not scared of flying, are you?"

"No, but I've been looking on the Internet. You want to know what I've found?"

"Not really," she said with a smile. "Ignorance is bliss; that's what Dad always says."

"The plane weighs forty-eight tons," Nicolai told her. "And it flies at a speed of five hundred and twenty-eight miles an hour. And when we get up to forty thousand feet, the temperature outside is minus sixty, and there are twenty-five tons of fuel in the tank. And if a flock of geese flies into the turbines, we're doomed. There have been eighteen major accidents involving this type of plane in which seven hundred and ninety people have died."

He looked at her and rolled his eyes, mostly to be funny. I'm glad he can still joke, Carmen thought, and laughed.

"Did you hear what I said? Seven hundred and ninety poor

people. Imagine," he said with a smile. "We might not survive. All that will be left of me is the filling in my bottom left jaw and a twisted skeleton. That's how they identify people. I mean, when there's nothing left apart from burned remains."

Carmen let out a peal of laughter, the one he had always loved and made him happy. She liked Nicolai's sense of humor and wanted to encourage him. "Jesus, Nicolai, you're not for real!"

They were sitting at a pizza bar waiting for their flight. Nicolai had not touched his food. A thought had just struck him and a deep, worried furrow appeared on his brow.

"I'm going to ask you something," he said earnestly. "And I want you to tell me the truth. Be absolutely honest, because I need to know for sure."

She looked at him and pouted, as she did when she was exasperated and impatient. "But I always give you an honest answer whenever you ask me anything," she said, slightly offended. She wiped her mouth with a napkin and looked at him askance.

"If they had done a test before" — he said in a very serious tone — "and told you that Tommy had Down syndrome, what would you have done? Would you have had an abortion?"

Carmen pushed the food away and thought for a few seconds. He didn't see any doubt and her voice was firm when she finally replied.

"Yes," she said, looking at him without shame. "Yes, I would have had an abortion. Which isn't that surprising. I'm more surprised that you asked. It's obvious, isn't it? No parent wants a child like that."

Nicolai crushed the napkin in his sweaty hand. "Yes, Carmen, they do," he said quietly. "I wanted Tommy. Just as he was."

"Yes, but Nicolai, now you have to be honest!" she persisted. "Would you really have wanted me to have him if we knew? With all the work and worry. For the rest of your life. A child that would never grow up. To have a young child in the house every day for the rest of your life? Would you really have wanted me to go through with it? I know they said at the hospital that people with Down syndrome had taken exams and passed their driving tests. But that's only a few. They're slow, Nicolai; they don't understand much at all!"

He balled his hands under the table, feeling his nails digging into his skin. More than anything he wanted to lash out. And he realized that if this conversation had taken place in the house at Granfoss, he would actually have hit her. He would have let rip because there was no one watching there. A desperate punch to the face, no going back. But the crowds of people drifting past the pizza bar made him stop. No, he thought the next second. I'm not someone who does that. I wouldn't sink that far; I have to get my act together.

"Now it's your turn to be honest," Carmen said sharply. "If we knew the truth before, should we have had Tommy?"

"Yes," Nicolai said. His voice was equally firm and without doubt. "We couldn't choose not to have a child just because he's not perfect. We're smarter than that, both of us. I mean, you're intelligent and so am I. And he must have inherited something from us. I mean, it's in the genes, even if he did have Down syndrome. Tommy would have managed, I'm positive. He would have passed his exams, and he would have gotten his driver's license. Because I would have made sure that he did all that. If only he'd lived. Do you hear what I'm saying?"

"But we'll never know," she said in a subdued voice and then stood up. She put her handbag over her shoulder and made to leave.

"Come on, let's go to the gate, and don't forget the whiskey and perfume. Boarding starts in five minutes. And please stop talking like that; it's too late anyway. We don't have the choice anymore."

28

"CONGRATULATIONS," CARMEN QUIPPED happily.

Nicolai put the suitcase down on the floor.

"For what?"

"We're here," Carmen said, "and you survived. All the bones in your body are intact; all your teeth are still there. It's great. Your heart is beating at the normal rate, and we're standing here and we're alive. Do you think we'll get back in one piece as well?"

He didn't answer. He wasn't scared of flying, despite his parents' fatal accident. He was just realistic—at least, that's how he saw it. Hotel San Rafael was an apartment hotel that was only about seven hundred feet from the long white beaches in Alcúdia. They had checked in and each been given a key card, and then taken the elevator up to the third floor. Carmen went in first and was over the moon about everything, especially the balcony that overlooked the Mediterranean and the big bedroom. And another room with a living area and a kitchen. There was a welcome basket on the counter with biscuits, grapes and wine, chocolate and nuts. Everything was clean and tidy, and the temperature was pleasant and cool. The air conditioning hummed faintly in the background. They went out onto the balcony. The Mediterranean glittered blue, and they could see a few boats far out on the horizon, some of them with full white sails.

"Nice," Nicolai said quietly. He leaned against the railing and looked down at the hotel garden. Carmen nodded happily. She slipped her arm around his waist and gave him an affectionate hug, wanting to be good and kind and patient for the whole week.

"We'll have some good days here, just you and me. Like it was before. I mean, before Tommy."

"But I don't miss the time before Tommy," he said. "Nothing happened in the time before Tommy. The time before Tommy just wasn't exciting."

"So I didn't make you happy," Carmen said, wounded. "Maybe you should have brought one of your old bikes with you instead," she teased. "Then you could have fiddled around with it out here on the balcony. Would you have been happier then, with an oil-can and overalls?"

"Yes," he said with a sad smile. "There's nothing like an old bike. Making everything work and turn."

She went back in and put the suitcase on the bed. She opened it and took out her clothes and hung them in the wardrobe. They had not packed much. If the suitcase was heavy, it was thanks to Carmen's toiletries. He never got used to the arsenal of bottles and pots. And she had of course brought her diary with her. She wanted to write in it every single day, so she could remember later what the vacation had been like. Nicolai was still sitting out on the balcony. He was curious about what she was writing, but he would never look, even though he had the chance—there was something about reading another person's diary. He suddenly felt nervous. His heartbeat was uneven and his palms were sweaty. It was like something was going to happen, only he didn't know what, like a premonition. Like a darkness growing in him that made him feel bleak. It wasn't just his grief for Tommy; there was something else there now. Something fateful and frightening. Like he was out of orbit and heading straight into the dark. These heavy thoughts made him feel like he was tossing and turning, even though he was sitting in a chair. He got up and went to the living room to find the duty-free bag and the bottle of whiskey. Then he got a glass from the kitchen cupboard. He poured himself a generous dram and went back out onto the balcony.

"You go easy now!" Carmen warned him.

"It's just one," Nicolai said testily. "I need it to calm my nerves; I've got so much to think about."

"No more than me," Carmen retorted. "We're in the same boat, aren't we? I just think whiskey's a bad solution, in the long run, at least."

"That's not true," Nicolai said. "Whiskey is in fact the best solution. Works every time."

Carmen took a bottle of water from the fridge and went out to keep him company.

"We'll manage this," she said with determination. "Listen to me. When the tragedy happened—when you came down to the pond and saw that Tommy was dead—you couldn't even speak then, couldn't think. And now we're having a conversation and soon we'll go out for some food. Everything passes, you'll see. And if you want to be in this world, you have to act like the living. It's an old Native American saying."

Nicolai drank some whiskey.

"Yes," he said, after some time. "But I'm not a Native American."

"No," Carmen laughed. "But let me pretend that you're my little Apache. And now you're fighting for Tommy. I understand that you want to hold on to the grief, but it doesn't help to wallow in all that suffering. So no more whiskey. Let's go out and enjoy the warm streets."

29

DEAR DIARY, I'VE got a lot on my mind.

We're far away now. Nicolai and I have left Granfoss behind, and we're in the sun and it's really warm. Nicolai keeps complaining. And the Majorcans? They whistle at me on the street wherever we go. It must be the blond hair. Because everyone is so dark here, I really stand out. There are still lots of tourists, even though it's the end of the season — loads of lobster-pink Englishmen and fat Danes. I keep trying to cheer up Nicolai, because he seems so down. He can't seem to settle, just sulks and wallows. I think it's a shame, because we could be having such a good time. But he just doesn't want to. I think about Tommy a lot, too, but I don't dwell on it. We have to move on. I insist on having another baby, a clever, bright little thing. I insist on living.

Every now and then I'm thrown by the fact that Tommy is gone forever. I can't understand it, no matter how hard I try. I mean, never to return. He's gone for the rest of human existence and won't come back in any shape or form. At least, I don't believe he will, but you never know. And one day I'll die too and be gone forever, and Nicolai will die. Everyone will disappear. It exhausts me to think about things like that too much. Sometimes I wonder about Nicolai, if he's maybe a bit too obsessed with death, because he's so sad. And sometimes I ask myself if I really love him. I have asked myself quite a lot in the past few days. And I don't think I do. This is not a good thing, because we're married. But then I'm not so sure he loves me. It's more like mutual sympathy. Even though we argue quite a lot, there is sympathy there. Or we're just together out of habit. But now that Tommy's gone, anything can happen. Maybe we'll fall apart. Maybe in the end we'll go our separate ways. It's not like I'm scared of the idea of divorce. If it happens, I'll get over it pretty quickly, because that's just the way I am. And in any case, there aren't many married couples who carry on loving each other year after year. I've seen that here on the streets of Alcúdia. Seen all the couples that are not together. They're in different worlds, and what their hearts are hiding must never come to light. The bitter secrets of some are revealed in their drawn mouths. With others it's the longing in their eyes, the dream of something else, something better. Everyone has that dream. No matter what we've got, everything could always be better. There are some who walk close together and look happy, like we were once happy. But lots of people sit together in silence and say nothing as they eat. It's quite depressing to admit that nothing is forever.

But I don't want to think about sad things. We've come here to forget, even though Nicolai sees it as letting Tommy down. He thinks our tragedy should fill our hearts every waking moment, but then we would be swallowed up and I won't let that happen. I've got a life to live and enjoy to the fullest. He's calling from the balcony now, so I have to stop. Goodbye for now, dear diary, it's so good to have you. I can think clearly on paper, which is such a relief. Nicolai's life is in chaos, I can tell. He wouldn't manage without me. I'm holding him up. He criticizes me for being happy, but he doesn't understand that one of us has to carry the load. Of course I think a lot about Tommy, but not all the time. He's out of my mind for long chunks, and then I feel peaceful and can see that life is worth living after all. Then I see Nicolai's bitter face and the grief hits me again like a punch in the stomach. But I'm strong and I can keep things together, keep Nicolai together.

30

TWENTY-FOURTH OF SEPTEMBER. Morning at Ågårds Plass.

"Yes," Dr. Morris said, "that's right. Carmen Cesilie Zita comes to me when she needs to. I've been her physician for more than four years now. Nicolai is also registered here, by the way, but he's never really been in. He's never ill. That's to say, he's thin and anemic, but there's nothing wrong with him. He's got a robust constitution. So yes, I know about Carmen's epilepsy; that's our main concern. It's almost fully under control now, but she does still have seizures every now and then. There's no denying it's a problem, but not on a day-to-day basis. And yes, I heard about her little boy. What a tragedy. I comfort myself with the thought that they're young and can start again, though I wouldn't dream of saying that to Miss Zita. It's a cold comfort. Things are no less painful when you're young. The opposite perhaps. But they can have more children, and I believe they will, given time, once they have mourned enough. I would give them a couple of years. In my experience, that's how long it takes."

"What is epilepsy?" Sejer asked. "Can you explain it to me? In a way that I can understand?"

Morris folded his hands on his desk. "Well," he started, "contrary to what most people think, epilepsy is not an illness, even

144

though many experience it as such. Let me put it this way: epilepsy is in fact the symptom of various conditions, all of which involve neurological disorders, which result in seizures, convulsions, and blackouts."

"A neurological disorder," Sejer repeated to himself. He was thinking about his own dizziness. Perhaps that was some form of neurological disorder. Then he thought, stop. Get a grip. You're here about something else.

"Yes, that's what we call it," Morris said. "And the causes of epilepsy can vary; it might be the result of a number of things. In around fifty percent of cases, the cause remains a mystery. But Carmen sustained brain injuries during birth and so has had epilepsy all her life, her young life, I should say. They were twins. One, Louisa, died at birth. She only lived an hour."

"What about Tommy's birth? Was the C-section planned, or was it an emergency?"

"It was planned," Morris confirmed. "Her pelvis is extremely narrow. It's almost a miracle that she could carry the baby to term. And despite having Down syndrome, he was a healthy baby."

"Can you tell me a bit about her seizures?"

Morris took off his glasses and fiddled with the arms. "Yes, of course. Carmen has what we call GTC seizures, that's to say generalized tonic–clonic seizures. These comprise two phases. In the tonic phase, the patient loses consciousness, which is dramatic enough in itself. The body then becomes rigid and the air is forced out of the lungs, which can sound like a scream and is very alarming for those present. Then the patient stops breathing and the face and lips turn blue. After a few seconds, the seizure then goes into the clonic phase, which causes the convulsions normally associated with epilepsy. The face turns red and the patient starts to breathe again."

"And how long does a seizure last?" Sejer asked.

"Oh, it varies considerably. As a rule, it's a matter of seconds and minutes. But sometimes the patient experiences a persistent series of seizures, one after the other, a condition that is called status epilepticus. Maybe you've heard of it? It is a very serious condition, and it is important to get the patient to the hospital as quickly as possible."

"Has Carmen ever suffered from status epilepticus?"

"Yes, she has. But only once since I've been her doctor, and it was pretty serious. She was kept in the hospital under observation for a couple of days. It's some time ago now, and I hope that she doesn't have to go through that again, because it is very stressful."

"And she is medicated now?"

"Yes, she's got medicine. And we're managing to keep seizures to a minimum. I would say she has a seizure about once a month, which is not so bad. She can live with that. But after a seizure, she can be rather out of it, confused and weak and tired."

"And how do you feel she copes with it? Is she bothered by it?"

Morris shook his head. "No, I wouldn't say that; she takes it in her stride. But then I've never really asked her directly. Even though she's a slip of a thing, she's tough as old boots. It's just awful what happened to the little boy. I heard about it on the news and was horrified. It's dangerous to live so close to water when you've got small children. How are they? I haven't seen them for a couple of months. It's a terrible tragedy to lose your child."

"It's actually Nicolai who's taking it the worst," Sejer told him. "As you said, Carmen is tough. She's the one who is coping best; she's forward-looking. She's talking about having another baby, so she's back in the driver's seat."

"And that's of little comfort for Nicolai," Morris said.

"Exactly, no comfort at all. He's taken this very badly. To be honest, I'm worried about him. And he's so alone, without any family."

"Excuse me for asking, but I'm curious," Morris started, leaning forward over his desk. "Why are you asking for information about Carmen's epilepsy? I mean, does it have anything to do with the child's death?"

"Yes, perhaps," Sejer said and stood up. He pushed the chair back into place and got ready to leave. "But I'm afraid I can't divulge that information; I'm sure you appreciate that. Let me just go back to something you said—that after a seizure, she is generally pretty out of sorts, tired and dizzy and weak."

"Yes," Morris replied. "In a language you no doubt understand, given your profession, after a major seizure she is in fact of unsound mind."

31

EVEN THOUGH IT was the end of the season, there were lots of people on Alcúdia's white beaches. But there was still plenty of room for Carmen and Nicolai. Carmen spread out their towels by the water's edge, pulled her sundress over her head, and stood there in her tiny red bikini. It made Nicolai think of a raspberry ripple lollipop. Carmen, his young wife, was so petite and pretty that the Majorcans all whistled enthusiastically wherever they went.

"Do you think I can go topless?" she asked.

Nicolai was shocked. "No, are you mad? Please. They're all Catholics down here, so don't do it. You might be reported. If you take off your top, I'm going back to the hotel."

"OK, boss," she said, giggling. "No need to panic. I was only asking. Haven't got much to show anyway," she said with a laugh. Even though Tommy was dead, she was in such a good mood. A little vacation in the sun and she's left all her sorrows behind, Nicolai thought sorely.

After she'd had a look around, Carmen settled on the towel. It was a big, thick beach towel with a picture of Bugs Bunny on it. She had folded her sundress and was using it as a pillow. Nicolai sat looking at the sparkling Mediterranean. Some children were playing in the shallows, while their parents kept watch from the sand, not letting them out of sight. They should have kept an eye on Tommy like that.

"I'm going to the kiosk," he said. "Do you want anything? Anything to eat or drink?"

"No, I'm fine, thanks," Carmen said. "You can get something for me later. But it's nice that you want to play gallant. We could pretend that we're on our honeymoon. We could pretend that we got married yesterday and are very happy. Please say yes, Nicolai," she said with a big smile.

He didn't answer. Honeymoon? They were mourning! How could she think like that? He got up and walked across the warm sand to the kiosk that stood in the shade between some trees. He placed his order and opened his wallet to pay. While he waited for the change, he turned around and looked at Carmen. It was strange to see her from a distance, in her red bikini. Everything became so clear: her beauty, her energy, the things he couldn't deal with. She seemed so untouched, and he couldn't understand it. Apparently unaffected by everything that had happened. Or, he thought, I'm merciless, mean, and without empathy. I think that I'm better than her and grieving more than her, that I was a better parent to Tommy. Shame on you, Nicolai. Shame on you!

He clenched his fist, exasperated with himself. Then he got his change and walked back and sat down on his towel. He opened the can of beer and took a swig. Carmen sat up and looked at him. Something caught her eye and she was taken aback.

"What are you doing? Why did you buy cigarettes?" She nodded at the pack of Marlboros lying on his towel, alongside an orange disposable lighter. "You don't smoke; why have you got Marlboros? Get a grip."

"I've just started," Nicolai retorted. "I'm starting right now. The way things are, I don't see any reason to stay healthy. I might as well enjoy what life's got to offer. Like you've always done, haven't you?"

His voice was harsh and desperate. He tore the plastic from the pack, fished out a cigarette, and lit it. He took a deep drag, pulled the smoke down into his lungs, and started to cough.

"Jesus Christ, how can you be so stupid?"

"It's none of your business," he said, irritated, and coughed again. "It's my life. If I want to ruin my lungs, I have every right to do so without you interfering."

"OK," Carmen said petulantly. "But I'm not going to kiss you when you've been smoking. It's disgusting."

"Fair enough," he said and took another drag on the cigarette. "We don't kiss very much anyway."

Carmen stood up and walked down to the water, paddled some way out, and then shouted back to him in excitement.

"It's almost like bathwater! Put that stupid cigarette out and come in!"

Nicolai wanted to finish his cigarette. He remained stubbornly where he was on the towel and took another drag. That's right, he thought. Let the smoke drown my lungs in tar. From now on, it's whiskey and cigarettes all day long. He found comfort in the idea of destroying himself. I deserve to be punished, he thought melodramatically. This is for Tommy.

"Come in, come and feel the water," Carmen encouraged him. "You can't sit there smoking all day."

He stubbed out the cigarette in the sand, got up, and waded out into the water. He dived in and then started to swim straight out.

"Don't go too far!" Carmen cried. "Stay close to the shore. I don't want to stand here shouting; please do as I say!"

He went a bit farther but then turned and swam back in toward her. He was an excellent swimmer and kept good pace. His swimming shorts stuck to his thighs and he had the taste of saltwater in his mouth. Everything was summer and sun and heat. Everything was never-ending sorrow. He was constantly switching between good and bad. For a while, he lay floating on his back. He enjoyed being cooled by the water, feeling fit and alive. After five minutes he got out again and went to sit on his towel.

"Can you put some sunscreen on my back?" Carmen asked. "It's in the bag."

He rummaged around and found the sunscreen. He sprayed it all over her back. Then he started to massage it into her skin. For a long time she lay there enjoying his touch in silence.

"Nicolai," she said. "I've been thinking about something. I've been thinking about it for a long time, since before Tommy died, just so you know. And we've talked about it before."

"OK," Nicolai said patiently. "What is it you want now?"

He massaged the lotion into the small of her back, right down to her bikini. But it gave him no pleasure—just flickering memories of better times, when they wanted each other.

"I've been thinking that maybe we should get a dog."

Nicolai stopped massaging. The idea left him speechless. Tommy was dead, and now she wanted a dog.

"But we have to go to work," he objected. "Sooner or later. And then the puppy will be left on its own all day. Do you really have the heart to do that? And you know how they are. They chew cables and things like that and have to be looked after all the time. No, we can't do it, Carmen. Drop it."

She put her head down on the towel again, determined she would convince him. He could tell she was giving it her all.

"All dogs are on their own during the day," she said. "Everyone has to go to work, don't they? We could take it for a little walk in the morning, so it can pee, and then go for a proper, longer work when we get home in the evening. Together, just the two of us. It would be so nice; the house is so empty now. Don't you think it's empty too?" she appealed. Her voice was reedy and pleading, a voice that was hard to resist. And he felt the hold she had over him, which made him give in like a helpless child.

He started to massage in the lotion again, slowly over her shoulders in circular movements. Her skin was like silk, golden-brown and smooth, without a blemish. She had a single mole in the small of her back, about the size of a thumbtack.

"A puppy costs thousands of kroner," he argued. "We can't afford it. I don't understand how you can even contemplate it when poor old Marian has to give us money all the time."

He was finished with the sunscreen, so he put it back in the bag and wiped his hands on the towel.

Carmen sat up again and brushed the sand from her feet. "Of course I can ask Dad," she said. "Dad will understand."

"OK," Nicolai said. "You get your way, as usual. What kind of dog were you thinking of? Please don't say a poodle. If you buy a poodle, I refuse to take it for walks."

Carmen burst out laughing. "No, I'm sure we can find something else. But it can't be too big or strong, because then I won't be able to deal with it. We can buy a dog book when we get home and I'm sure we'll find one we agree on. But OK, not a poodle. What have you got against them anyway?"

"Poodles are for old ladies," Nicolai said. He took out another cigarette and lit it.

"I don't get you, to start smoking like that, for no reason," Carmen complained.

In the evening, they sat on the balcony and stared out into the dark. Nicolai took drags on a cigarette and released long curling ribbons of smoke. She couldn't understand why he was smoking and what he was thinking, but she didn't want to get into an argument. Not now, when she was dreaming about their puppy. She needed to keep him sweet, and she knew how to do that.

"It's a lot of work keeping a dog," Nicolai said and took a sip of whiskey.

"But no more tiring than it was looking after Tommy," she said, "and we managed that fine, didn't we? Just think of all the energy it gave us. You never complained; you were wonderful."

He didn't answer. It had been tiring with Tommy, but it had given him nothing but pleasure from start to finish. Carmen drank some of her Coke, which was pretty flat now. She thought of Nicolai as clay, a mass that she could form as she wanted. Well, that's certainly how it had been for a long time. But now, since Tommy's death, he had become more obstinate. His new opposition annoyed her immensely. Latin American rhythms and happy sounds could be heard from the hotel garden: the tinkling laughter of women, the monotone rumble of men's voices, and the clinking of glasses. Carmen wanted to go downstairs and join in, but Nicolai wasn't interested. He couldn't dance either, so there was no point. He poured himself another whiskey and put the bottle down again with a thump.

"Make sure you don't drink too much now," she commanded. "I don't want to have to drag you around when you're drunk."

He didn't say anything, just lifted his glass. Part of him wanted to be left alone, but the other part was boiling, looking for a fight. There was so much he wanted to say to her, if only he dared. He felt a coward for not confronting her, but he knew from experience that she quickly got the upper hand. And when she ran out of arguments, she just started crying. And he couldn't cope with her crying now. He couldn't face an argument. Dog or no dog, it was all irrelevant. When I can't cope anymore, I give up, he thought, and I don't give a toss what other people think. Carmen will win this round too. I always knew she would. I'm pathetic. I play second violin. Dammit.

"Let's take the bus into Palma tomorrow," she said enthusiastically. "Then we can look at the shops."

"Yes, why not?" he said in a tired voice. He was clutching the glass, only thinking of one thing now, and that was getting drunk.

"And we can go to the cathedral," she continued. "Maybe we could light a candle there for Tommy."

Yes, it would be good to light a candle for Tommy. But it wouldn't ease the pain. His grief was like a millstone around his neck, pulling him down deeper and deeper. He felt the whiskey soothing him. He was floating away from reality. He thought, it's not true that he drowned. This is just a nightmare. And tomorrow I'll wake up and be happy in a new world.

"What do you think it's like here in autumn and winter?" Carmen asked.

"Dead," Nicolai replied. "Closed shops and empty beaches, cloudy and wet. People wandering around without any real purpose."

"Oh, come on, stop being silly. What do you think they live off?"

"Some of them probably have other jobs. And some probably live off what they earn in the summer. Think of all the tips you'd get in just one day. You're too generous with your tips, by the way, Carmen. You have to stop because we can't afford it."

The band down in the hotel garden had taken a break. All they could hear were the cicadas and the odd burst of laughter rolling out into the dense Mediterranean night. A horse-drawn carriage trotted past and they heard the horseshoes ringing out on the narrow cobbled street.

"I don't like greyhounds," she said out of the blue. "They're so thin. I don't like Alsatians because they always look so aggressive.

And I don't like bulldogs because they're ugly. I can't see how they manage to eat with their teeth the way they are. And you don't want a poodle. And I don't want one either. And Chihuahuas are too small; there are limits. St. Bernards are too big and setters are too nervous. And dachshunds have such short legs that they just look weird. I say we get a terrier. You know, one of those small ones. Come on," she said enticingly, "let's go to bed, it's late. I suggest a Jack Russell, a boy. They're the right kind of size and they look cool. You can't drink any more whiskey now; otherwise you'll feel like garbage. Remember we're going into Palma tomorrow, so you have to be in reasonable shape."

She stood up and went into the bathroom to brush her teeth. Nicolai stayed where he was out in the dark, sipping his whiskey. He didn't pay attention to Carmen's commands anymore. He was on a slippery slope. He was losing control. Again, all he felt was indifference. Indifference about the dog, indifference about going into Palma the next day. He sat out there for an hour and listened to the voices down in the garden, which were by now only a faint mumble. Finally he went into the bedroom. A dog, he thought, a little terrier. Why not? Something to pet, he thought, as he crept in under the comforter. Carmen was sleeping heavily. Sweaty and warm and soft, she was like a radiator after a day in the sun. But he didn't touch her. They hadn't touched at all since Tommy died.

32

THEY WALKED HAND in hand around the cathedral and lit a candle for Tommy. There was something wretched about the whole thing. You put a euro into the slot, like putting money in a piggy bank, and then a little bulb lit up. They stood there, filled with emotion, looking at the weak, energy-saving light.

"Do you think it will stay lit until the evening?" Carmen asked hopefully.

"No, I doubt it will be more than a measly hour," Nicolai remarked. "Everyone wants to make money. The church is no exception. Tomorrow we'll have to put another euro in. Come on, it's nothing more than a little dirty bulb, so let's not get things out of proportion."

They sat in a pew and held hands. Carmen gave a little squeeze; she wanted so much to be kind. There were several other tourists in the church talking in hushed voices, a gentle murmur of different languages. Silence, prayer, and respect, for life and death. Their heads and hearts filled with the thought that there was perhaps more than this wretched daily toil with its suffering and grief. Nicolai liked the dim, beautiful interior. The church gave him a sense of peace. He could sit there forever in the hard pew and stare at the weak light from Tommy's candle.

Time passed and eventually they dragged themselves away and continued to explore the town. They went up to the main square, Plaza Major, where they found a bar. They each ordered a beer and sat and sipped it in the shade of the trees, looking out at the square and the passersby. A fountain splashed ice-cold water in front of the august buildings that lined the plaza. There were stalls selling all manner of things: flowers, fruit and vegetables, baskets and colorful shawls. As Nicolai enjoyed his beer, he thought about Carmen as he observed her surreptitiously over the edge of his glass: her golden skin, her slim hands fidgeting restlessly on the table. He knew that if he left her, if he actually did what he was thinking about, she would grieve for a few weeks and then she would settle into her new situation, adaptable as she was. He would of course have to move out of Granfoss. After all, it was Marian who had bought the house for them. And where would he go? He would also have to find himself another job. He couldn't carry on working at Zita Quick if he was going to leave Carmen. That would be impossible. Jesus, he thought, I'm trapped. If he was going to leave, he would have to go far away, beyond the reach of all the tears and accusations. People saying that he was a worrier, as Carmen always claimed. A weak and helpless soul who couldn't move on. He took a sip of beer and looked over at the other tourists; they all looked so happy, wearing shorts and sandals. Children's laughter, ice cream, pigeons pecking at crumbs in the cobbled square. Meanwhile he was drowning in grief, gasping for air, desperately trying to force his heart to keep a normal speed. Down in the harbor, which they had passed on the way to the cathedral, he could see rows and rows of luxury boats: *Doris*, *Fortuna*, and *Paradise*. There were a few for sale. If you had a boat, he thought, you could just sail away from everything, out to the curve of the horizon.

The waiter came over to their table with a bowl of salted pistachio nuts. Nicolai put one in his mouth.

"Are you sad?" he asked suddenly. The words fell out of his mouth before he could think. Carmen raised an eyebrow and stared at him uncertainly.

"I don't know what you mean."

"Don't be stupid," he snapped. "Tommy drowned in Damtjern on August 10. And I'm asking if you're finding it hard. You don't look like you're sad. What are you actually thinking?" he asked, banging his beer glass down on the table. Beer splashed over the edges, and a sudden indignation flared up inside him.

"What do you mean?" she said, still hesitating. "Stop playing around."

"You know perfectly well what I mean. And what were you thinking when you carried him down to the pond? I can't believe that you stood there on the jetty and threw him into the water. What if someone had seen you? What if people didn't believe your crazy explanation?"

She picked up her glass and took a couple of greedy gulps. Again, her cheeks were flushed, as if he had caught her lying.

"I've given my explanation," she said. "I was terrified. I was scared that I would be blamed and I couldn't face that because it was an accident."

"An accident. Yes, rather convenient that you have epilepsy."

She leaned over the table. They sat and glared at each other, neither of them wanting to back down. Nicolai's stubborn green eyes stared straight into her blue ones. Her defiance grew in the face of his accusation.

"What are you trying to prove?" she asked. "What are you going on about? I've told the truth and I've got nothing more to say about Tommy's death. You really are pushing it now. I don't want any more accusations. I was the one who looked after Tommy. You were at work, and you weren't there most of the time. I'm the one who had to answer all the questions. About what he could and couldn't do, about his future, about why he was so slow, why he didn't understand what we said to him. It hasn't been easy, you know. I was pretty desperate at times. And you've damn well always been on the outside."

"Yes," he said. "I was at work. One of us had to keep the money coming in. If you thought looking after him was so difficult, you should have said so. We could have swapped for a while; you could have worked at Zita Quick for as long as you liked. I even said as much, but you didn't want to listen."

"That's easy for you to say," she said, "because you're fit and healthy. You don't need to worry about suddenly keeling over. But let me tell you, it's not great to live with. And I don't feel particularly proud of myself either, about what's happened. I admit that I did try to change my story, because I was terrified of being charged with negligence. It's not damn easy knowing what the police are going to do. Everyone's out to get me; you could at least be on my side. I've wept buckets too, so there."

"Yes, you're certainly good at crying," he said. "You turn on the waterworks whenever it suits you. But I've cried too. And the only comfort I have is some fantastic story about a moment's confusion. You owe it to me to explain how you could think of doing something like that. Throwing a baby into the water to cover something you claim was an accident is just crazy. Honestly."

Carmen finished her beer, and then she too banged her glass down on the table. Her mouth was drawn and pale, despite the sun.

"You should be damn grateful that you don't have epilepsy,"

she said in a bitter voice. "You don't have to lie unconscious on the floor in spasms. And then come to again without being able to remember anything. Everything is just a blind spot in your head. Yes, I know it was stupid. But it's too late for regret, and Tommy's death was an accident. So why can't you just believe me and be done!"

Nicolai sat back and crossed his arms. "Not strange really, that the police keep questioning you," he said calmly. "You've spun them a pretty good story. Think about when you're in court. How will you get them to believe anything so far-fetched?"

"They'll believe me because it's the truth," she said. "Simple as that." She finished the last of her beer and looked at him with pleading eyes. "Can we just for once be honest? I didn't think it was much fun that Tommy turned out the way he did. That I would always have to deal with his problems."

"What do you mean, problems?"

"Don't make yourself out to be more stupid than you are. You know perfectly well what I mean. He would never be able to keep up in life. I would always have to explain to other people why my child wouldn't do what was expected of a child his age. People are nosy and ask so many questions. Yes, I've got a son, but unfortunately he's an idiot. I think you should apologize. I can't believe you would accuse me of lying. Fuck you for being so self-righteous. I've got a lot of stuff going on inside as well. And it's not as if you don't have any faults."

"I don't trust you," he said and drank some more beer. Again he banged his glass on the table. "If you're sitting there hiding a terrible secret, I hope it eats away at you from inside."

Carmen stood up and put her bag over her shoulder. Then she took her empty glass and threw it down onto the asphalt with all her might, so the glass shattered. "There you go," she snarled. "You can tidy it up."

As she walked away across the cobbled square, she shouted over her shoulder to him: "I'm going back to the hotel. And this argument never happened."

33

DEAR DIARY,

The week is nearly over, it's gone so fast. What am I going to do with Nicolai? Today he was so suspicious and I don't know what to say. I have to watch myself every second of the day. I have to weigh my words. Because I need him to be on my side. We're both going to court in June, and I need him to be my witness, to stand up for me. But he doesn't seem to care about anything anymore. Doesn't care about the future, doesn't think about our case going to court and that we'll have to be there. The only thing he thinks about is feeding his grief and the loss of Tommy, keeping the wound open at all costs. He smokes and drinks whiskey, sits out on the balcony and cries. I can't bear it. And if I ask him something, his answers are monosyllabic and he's not interested. Sometimes he gives me long, suspicious looks, I suppose to show that he doesn't trust me.

I've been thinking a lot about death recently.

Death as final and terrible, death as merciless. But also death as gentle. And about God, though I don't actually believe in Him. But sometimes I'm gripped by the thought that one day we will all be laid out in white in a cold grave—that damp black hole in the earth is waiting for us all. The worms and other creepy-crawlies will make their way in through the coffin and slowly we are eaten by the tiny teeth of time. But sometimes incredible things happen. Things that turn our ideas upside down. One day last November, I gave some money to a beggar. I don't usually do that, because it goes against my principles. People have to find a way to make ends meet, isn't that an obligation we all have? So it was just a whim. Just because it seemed right at the time. God bless you, the beggar said gratefully. I gave him a hundred-kroner note and his pale eyes filled and shone with tears. And right then, for that moment, when he said those words, I became deeply religious. I did not doubt for a moment that I would be blessed. A sudden warmth spread through my body and I felt like I was floating and light as a feather. Anything that was weighing me down slipped away and I loved everyone. I saw them so clearly as they walked toward me on the pavement. For the rest of the day I wandered around in this state of bliss, held on to the feeling. I wanted it to last forever. Fate had given me the chance to be a good person. But the days passed and doubt crept back, and my memory of the beggar lost its significance. Nothing lasts forever. I know that better than anyone. And then, dear diary, last night I had a horrible dream. That's what I wanted to tell you, because it was so awful. I dreamed that we went to bed in our house up at Granfoss. It was late at night. I went to check that Tommy was OK first, like I normally did. But as I stood there looking at him, he started to scream. Nicolai immediately wanted to have him in our bed. He can't lie there on his own, screaming like that, he said. I can't stand it, it drives me crazy. Because when he cries it means that there's something he doesn't have.

Yes, I said, obviously there's something he doesn't have. He doesn't have intelligence, and you'll only spoil him if he gets everything he wants the minute he makes a noise. He's a baby, Nicolai, and they tend to cry over nothing. But Nicolai totally disagreed. He wanted to lift the boy up and comfort him. Come on, he'll stop any moment, I said, convinced, and he's going to sleep in his own room now. We can't carry on like this and let the baby turn us out of our own bed. I'll go crazy soon as well, I exclaimed, with all this fuss!

As we stood there arguing by the crib, his screaming really started to get on our nerves. He screamed like his lungs were fit to burst. It was intense and piercing, and his face was bright red with sweat and effort. We left him and got into our double bed, but it was impossible to sleep as Tommy continued to cry at full volume. I wanted to leap out of bed and with all my might shake his little body into silence. After a couple of minutes we gave up. Nicolai pushed the comforter to one side and went over to the crib. Come and look! he shouted, obviously agitated. Tommy's grown! He's so big he almost doesn't fit! Reluctantly I got out of the warm bed and went over to see what he meant. And then to my horror I saw that Tommy was enormous. See, Nicolai said. He doesn't fit anymore, so we'll have to move him.

So Nicolai got what he wanted. I lifted Tommy out of the crib and he was so heavy that I only just managed to carry him. And then finally he was in our bed. And finally he stopped crying. I turned my back to him and closed my eyes, praying for some peace and quiet. But then, just as we were about to fall asleep, he started to cry again, and by now Nicolai was desperate. Look, he said, Tommy's still growing. And when I turned over, I froze. Because Tommy was so big now that there almost wasn't room for him. And as I lay there in the bed staring at him, he started to change color and slowly his body was covered by a gray, almost silvery shell. And then it dawned on me that Tommy had turned into a fish. I screamed at Nicolai in a panic, get him away from me! Get him away!

Before I knew it, I had been squeezed over the edge of the bed.

I woke up on the floor. But I was OK, despite the nightmare, because it was only a dream and I've always been a fighter. We're going home tomorrow, and I can't help but hope things will get back to normal again, even though it all seems pretty bleak at the moment. We'll manage to sort things out, Nicolai and me. I've always been an optimist. I have so many nights ahead of me, hopefully without dreams about death. I know that Nicolai lies awake while I sleep like a log, exhausted by the sun and heat that they have so much of down here. Sometimes I say the Lord's Prayer. It can't do any harm and I need to find support somewhere, even if I am strong.

I called good night to Nicolai, who is sitting on the balcony drinking. Taking the edge off your desperation with whiskey is a slippery slope and I'm very worried. Tomorrow he'll be morose, slow, and hung-over. It doesn't bother him in the slightest. It's me who has to keep it all together and sort everything out, but I get tired sometimes.

It's nighttime, so I'm going to go to bed now. And there's no Tommy there, taking up space, no scaly fish. I'm sorry to say it, dear diary, but I've already got used to him not being there. No matter how hard I try, I cannot feel any real deep despair. Tommy was hard work. I was ashamed of Tommy. He was a great disappointment. My hopes were for something completely different when I was pregnant. In the old days, the parents were blamed. A handicapped child was a punishment from a reprimanding God, and if that really is the case I can only apologize. I haven't lived a life free of sin, but nor has anyone else, so there. No matter what, I want to start over again. With a strong, healthy child, because I deserve it. Why shouldn't I get what everyone else does? I'll call

Nicolai one last time, but he doesn't want to hear. And God only knows I'm trying to help. Maybe he's right, maybe everything will just go to hell, but then he can deal with it on his own. I refuse to sacrifice my life for him, and charity begins at home. Isn't that what they say?

34

TENTH OF OCTOBER. Night.

In among all the mess and files in his study, Sejer found some old court papers that piqued his curiosity. He took them, settled back down by the window, and started to read while he sipped at a generous dram of whiskey.

Annie ruthlessly suffocated her daughter, who was only four years old. The killing is a tragedy and completely senseless. There are many special and apparently inexplicable circumstances attached to the event, and during the case several possible motives, or things that might have triggered the murder, were presented.

Annie and her daughter, Beate, were alone at home. In the course of the afternoon, a friend, who was also four, came to play and then left around bedtime. Beate had a lot of fun and was over-excited. The friend was collected by her mother, who estimated that she got there just after seven o'clock. She and her daughter left about ten minutes later. At 7:34, the emergency services control center received a phone call from an apparently hysterical Annie who said that Beate had stopped breathing. It was a very dramatic exchange and the mother was screaming in panic. She was instructed to administer heart compressions and mouth-to-mouth until the ambulance arrived just under ten minutes later. The doctor got there five minutes after that. Attempts to revive the little girl were unsuccessful and stopped after three-quarters of an hour.

The accused has the following history: In autumn 2002, Annie suffered from severe depression that resulted in her being admitted to the Østmarka Ward, St. Olav's Hospital: a psychiatric institution. The record of her psychiatric illness proved to be long and of a complex nature, stretching over many years. Her childhood and puberty involved many difficulties. It was suspected that she suffered from dysthymia, with severe depressive episodes. She herself thought she suffered from a bipolar disorder, although a diagnosis of borderline (emotionally unstable) personality disorder had also previously been suggested—the diagnosis now finally given by forensic psychiatrists.

With regard to sentencing, the objective aggression and nature of intent shall be central. The accused's personal circumstances and difficulties must come second. She has no psychological condition or altered state of consciousness that would warrant her reaction.

And for want of other confirmed grounds, the High Court judgment must be based on the more lenient alternative for the accused. That is to say, an impulsive act, or a crime of passion, such that the killing of Beate was a result of a situation or moment that provoked an aggressive outburst. The accused lost control in a confrontation with the child. In all probability this was triggered by something minor and a screaming, difficult child, and it is not possible for the court to establish extenuating circumstances. The accused's personality disorder with associated mood swings and aggressive outbursts may serve as an explanation, but it does not provide sufficient extenuating circumstances to influence the punishment. The victim was a small defenseless child who was in her mother's care in her own home. In such circumstances, a child has the right to absolute safety.

The injuries indicate that the child had been subjected to considerable physical force, both before and during suffocation. Based on the findings described in the autopsy report and the known criteria for death by suffocation, it is most probable that Beate's airways were obstructed by hands being held to her nose and mouth. The findings indicate the use of aggressive force.

Being suffocated must have been a terrifying experience for the child. It is assumed that death occurred after ninety seconds, and every single one of those seconds would have involved struggle and torment. It is assumed that the accused held Beate in a firm grip and that the child fought back as much as possible, but in vain, given her inferior physique. The accused must have maintained her hold until there was no way back, and Beate finally fell into a coma and stopped breathing. The accused therefore had the opportunity to regain composure. With regard to sentencing, it must therefore be emphasized that the victim was a defenseless young child in the accused's care. The court must also take into consideration the aggravating circumstances that followed the incident: the accused's attempt to cover up the crime and denial of it by fabricating an alternative course of events.

An alternative course of events, Sejer thought to himself. That was more or less what Carmen had said. And there certainly were many plausible and implausible explanations. Such as an epileptic seizure, followed by severe confusion and an inability to judge. Of course it was an accident. I lost consciousness and afterward it was too late; the child slid down in the bathtub and under the soapy water. An old story whose hallmarks were familiar to him after so many years at the station in Søndre District: the manipulation, denial, explanations, and lies. He had heard so many stories in his time with the police, as if panic in itself made the perpetrator insane. Normal rules no longer applied when you were furious; your body was flooded with adrenaline and a hot glowing rage that made your blood boil. Sejer put the papers down and drank what was left of the whiskey. He leaned back in his chair and closed his eyes, thinking about little Beate and her tragic fate. Annie was sentenced to eleven years in prison. Then he thought about Carmen and how she would cope inside, if the case ended in a conviction. Beautiful, spoiled little Carmen. Who had possibly killed her own son in a moment of desperation. Or rage. Or was it something else, something worse, which he could not bear to think about. Yet he could not ignore it, as it continued to pop up from time to time as a possible scenario. The thought that it might be murder, premeditated in detail. The boy wasn't like other children. He was a burden, a child she didn't like others to see.

He put the leash on the dog and started to walk down the stairs from the twelfth floor. A door closed and he heard footsteps. This made Frank stop and listen, and then he continued his descent. All was still outside, not a breath of wind in the trees. It was mild, maybe 60 degrees. What an amazing summer it had been, he mused, but it was definitely over. Now the storms would come, the cold and rain. Frank tugged at his leash, sniffed a soft banana skin, and abandoned it. He moved on, his sensitive black nose sniffing his way around. Nicolai has nothing to do with this, Sejer thought. No, he is certainly not involved in any way. But why am I so certain? They could have done it together. In which case, my intuition is worth nothing.

He wandered aimlessly, allowing Frank to sniff around for quite some time. In the middle of the square in front of the building, which was full of parked cars, Sejer stood and looked up at the stars twinkling in the sky. They say it's written in the stars, he mused. How convenient it would be if I could find the answer there. Frank tugged at the leash again and then trotted back toward the block of apartments. On the way he decided to leave his mark one last time, on the wheel of a blue Golf.

"Come on," Sejer said, heading toward the entrance. He crossed the square with brisk steps, punched in the code, and opened the heavy wired-glass door. He left his thoughts outside in the dark and plodded back up the stairs to the twelfth floor. It was there, as he turned onto the last landing, that he suddenly stopped. It was past midnight. Nearly everyone was in bed asleep. But Frank pulled at the leash and started to quiver. Nicolai Brandt was sitting on the top step.

Sejer stood there for a moment, staring in surprise. Then he mounted the final few steps and held out his hand. "Nicolai. Is something wrong? What's up?"

The lad stood and backed toward the wall. For a moment, it seemed that he regretted coming, that he wanted to flee. But he stayed where he was all the same.

"How did you get in?" Sejer asked.

"I rang all the bells; it usually works. I shouldn't have come," he said despondently.

Sejer fished his keys out of his pocket and unlocked the door. He opened it and put his hand on Nicolai's shoulder.

"Come on in, then we can talk. I presume you've got something you want to say, something important. And I've got more than enough time, so come on in."

Frank jumped up and danced around, but Nicolai showed no interest. He came hesitantly into the hall and took off his sneakers with dirty laces. He wore a hoodie with a picture of Mick Jagger on it, and his thin hair was combed back from his forehead.

"We've been away; we were in Majorca for a week," he explained. "If you tried to get hold of us, that is."

"Yes," Sejer said. "I spoke to your father-in-law. It wasn't anything important. I hope you had a good time. Why don't you go and sit down over by the window. I'll put some coffee on."

"Not for me, thanks. There's no need. I've just got something quick to say, and then I'll be on my way." He walked farther into the living room and looked around at the furniture to get his bearings in the unfamiliar, tidy room.

"I know that the case is due to come up in June," he said. "Friis told us that we'll both be called as witnesses about events on August 10. And if I've understood right, I have to go to court. If I don't show up, they'll come to collect me."

He didn't say any more, just dug his hands into his pockets. He shifted his weight from one foot to the other, then stood there. He swayed slightly, restless.

"Yes," Sejer confirmed, "that's right. It's the law. Tell me what's on your mind. Is there anything I can do?"

Nicolai rubbed his eyes; he seemed exhausted.

"No. I'm not going to be a witness in court. You can say what you like. That's why I'm here. I want to do it now."

"Sit yourself down," Sejer said again. "What do you mean, you're not going to be a witness? We both know that you're legally bound to do so."

Nicolai finally sat down in a chair. His hands gripped the armrests so hard his knuckles were white.

"So, what have you got to tell me?" Sejer prompted. "I'm all ears."

"You mustn't believe a word Carmen says," Nicolai said insistently.

Sejer gave the lanky youth a grave nod. He'd gotten some color in Majorca and his cheeks were red. "Let me just make one thing absolutely clear," Sejer told him. "Whatever you say now can be used against you. How far are you prepared to go? Do you know any more than that, that's she not telling the truth?"

Nicolai reached out and scratched Frank behind the ear. "I don't know what happened," he said, "and I'm not going to accuse her of anything. But I don't believe the story that she told. And I don't want to say anything else. It's your job to find out the truth. I just wanted to let you know that she has a vivid imagination. That's to say, a damn vivid imagination."

He ran his fingers through his hair again in a nervous manner.

"Perhaps you could answer one simple question?" Sejer ventured. "In your opinion, did she love Tommy? I mean, was there a strong bond between them? Were they close?"

"Of course they were," he said hastily. "But the one doesn't rule out the other. Yes, I do think she loved him. And I do think she misses him, every now and then at least. But I don't think she regrets anything. That's to say if she has done anything terrible."

"When you say terrible, what do you mean?" Sejer asked.

"I think you understand," he said curtly. "Use your imagination."

Sejer gave him a piercing look. "That's a very serious accusation, Nicolai, but you're no doubt aware of that."

"Give me an honest answer," Nicolai responded. "Do you believe Carmen's story? Or do you think she's lying, like I do?"

"I don't want to answer that. But of course I have a number of theories. Let's just hope that we can find the real story. Let's hope we find a solution that you can both live with, despite the terrible tragedy."

"No, I'll never be able to live with this. You have to do your job. If Carmen is lying, it's your job to find out. So what do you think? Will the jury believe her story about having an epileptic fit?"

"Quite possibly, yes. And even though you have your suspicions, you have to face up to the fact that the story might be true. I've been wrong before," Sejer said, "and perhaps you have too."

"Yes, I've been wrong. But not this time." He looked around the living room and noticed all of the photographs on the wall. He stood up and went closer to look at them. "Your wife?" he asked and pointed. Elise beamed down at him with her beautiful smile.

Sejer nodded.

"And who's the ballet dancer?"

"My grandson," Sejer said. "He's in the National Ballet."

"That means he's good then."

"It does indeed."

"Is he adopted?"

"Yes, from Somalia. Come and sit down again. Don't change the subject."

Nicolai sank back down in the chair. "Carmen is like a piano string; she never breaks." He stood up abruptly and headed toward the door. "You won't get any more from me. I've said enough already."

He put on his shoes. Sejer gave up and followed him out to the door and opened it.

"What you have told me is very serious indeed," he said. "It's the kind of information that I am duty-bound to follow up on. So you have jeopardized the future for both you and Carmen."

"You're only saying what you have to say," Nicolai replied. "But that's fine, I know what I'm doing. I just want everything to be right, and I'm sure you agree."

He started to walk toward the elevator. Then he turned for a last time. "You'll never get a clearer explanation," he said. "Carmen can wriggle like a worm. And I know you need proof. But I still have hope, and remember that I know her. Maybe, sooner or later, she'll make a mistake."

35

ELEVENTH OF OCTOBER. Morning at Granfoss.

Nicolai was already up, but Carmen hadn't noticed him getting out of bed. What did he do last night, she wondered. He had gotten into the car and driven off, without any drama. Let me be, he'd said as he left. Eventually she'd given up waiting and had gone to bed around midnight. It was seven in the morning now, and she lay there for a little longer, dozing while she mulled over the situation. This strange life without Tommy. She wasn't used to the peace and quiet in the house, but it was good, she thought. She had to be honest. The new day lay ahead of her for her to use as she wished; she had an ocean of time. She lay completely still in the bed and listened for noises in the other rooms. The house felt empty, even though Nicolai was up. She could hear the air in the bedroom humming gently in the silence. And she imagined that the humming was the sound of the universe and all the planets spinning in their orbits.

Suddenly she felt hungry. Maybe he had made breakfast for her. One could always hope; he was a nice boy. Shy, reserved, modest, and sometimes downright slow. But a good boy. That was why she had chosen him. He never argued and never hit her. But now, after Tommy had died, he'd changed. She didn't really believe he'd made her breakfast; he was so indifferent to everything now. And his indifference worried her. He wasn't himself, wasn't the Nicolai she knew. She threw the comforter to one side and put her feet down on the cold floor. Then she went over to the window and looked out; it was a clear October day. She walked into the bathroom and turned on the faucet. She washed her face and popped a Rivotril in her mouth as she always did. Then she pulled a sweater over her head and went out into the kitchen, padding quietly on bare feet, and continued on into the living room.

The sofa was empty. The throw was neatly folded, so he hadn't slept there. Maybe he hadn't slept at all last night. Well, presumably he's in the cellar as usual, she thought. She prepared for this explanation, that he was down there tinkering with a bike. It was a safe bet. God knows what's so great about being in the dimness with all those old bikes, she thought, but then she realized it was only seven o'clock. Surely he couldn't be busy this early in the morning? She stood for a moment in the middle of the room, not sure what to do. Then she went back into the kitchen and got the butter, jam, and cheese out of the fridge. She put on the kettle and cut some bread, and set the table for a simple breakfast. When the water had boiled, she went out into the hall to the cellar door. She opened it and called down that breakfast was ready. But no one answered, so she closed the door again and went outside.

The Golf was parked beside the mailbox. She looked over toward the pond but couldn't see him. He must have gone for a walk, she thought. But then again, it was very early. Going for a walk at seven in the morning was not very likely. The prospect of the puppy filled her with joy. They had just ordered one from a breeder in Oslo. A Jack Russell. They would go and collect it when it was eight weeks old, and she was so looking forward to it. Pappa Zita had given them his blessing, but then she had expected nothing less. Autumn would pass, and winter and spring, and then in the summer she would go to court and explain how Tommy had died. She didn't like to think too much about the court case. She mentally pushed it to one side. She knew that she would manage; she had great faith in her abilities and talents. She decided to weep copiously, because tears were always good. And, after all, what had happened was tragic, and the jury would be sympathetic. She was sure of it. One hundred percent certain.

I am Carmen Zita, she thought; don't even think about it! She tried not to worry about Nicolai. If he wanted to carry on this way, well then she'd let him. Smoking and drinking whiskey—what next? Sooner or later he would no doubt see sense and once again become the good old Nicolai she had fallen in love with. She wouldn't leave him. It would always be the two of them. If only he would sort himself out. If only he would come for breakfast.

When she was finished, she left everything on the table. That way it would be easy for him to have his breakfast when he got back from his walk. She put her glass and plate by the sink and then went into the bathroom. She pulled on a pair of jeans and looked at herself in the mirror. She stood there for a while studying her face, and she liked what she saw. It pleased her every time. She went back out to the kitchen and dialed Nicolai's cell number, only to hear it ringing in the bedroom. She found it on his bedside table, where it lay playing its happy tune. One missed call, she read on the display. OK, he didn't want to be reached and she had to respect that. She put on her shoes and went out into the yard and down to the pond. She sat at the end of the jetty, where Nicolai would sit for hours on end. She started to mull over life and the unexpected turns it had taken, things she hadn't planned. Things that she had no control over, like now. She shed some bitter tears because life was so hard, but she liked crying. She felt it was good to release the build-up of pressure inside. She pulled her cell phone out of her pocket and called her father.

"Everyone grieves differently," he said. "He just needs some space. You know he's not as strong as you are; he's so sensitive."

"He could at least have left a message," she said. "He just doesn't care anymore."

"Would you like me to come over?"

"No," she replied. "It's OK, he'll turn up."

"Of course he will," her father assured her. "He decides on his own life; there's not a lot you can do about it. But promise me that you'll call when he does come back, just so I know that everything's all right."

She promised. She finished the call and got up, walked back to the house, and went into the living room. Then she noticed his cigarettes on the coffee table, along with his lighter. She was surprised that he hadn't taken them with him, because it had become a habit now. He smoked all the time. She dismissed it and sat down at the desk. She opened the drawer and took out her diary to write a quick entry. "Dear diary, Nicolai has disappeared and it's early in the morning. I hope he's not crying somewhere. It would be better if he did that at home with me. Everything is just worse when you're on your own."

She didn't manage to write any more.

She called her father for the second time, and he got in the car right away. He was at her door half an hour later, stroking her gently on the cheek.

"More to worry about, eh?" he said. "As if you didn't have enough already. But you know what, he'll turn up. Just you wait and see. Come, let's go and look for him. Maybe he's gone down to Stranda; he likes being by the water. What do you think?"

She nodded and stood up straight. Yes, of course he'd gone

down to Stranda. She should have thought of that before. She left the door unlocked in case he hadn't taken his keys with him. She couldn't be sure. Suddenly she couldn't be sure about anything.

"Shall we take the car?" her father asked.

"No," Carmen said. "We'll walk; it will give him a bit more time. Then, when we get home, I'll give him what for."

"Well, it's certainly a lovely day," Pappa Zita said. "Nothing bad can happen when nature is on our side. And the October sky is blue and not a cloud to be seen, which must be a good sign."

"Dad, this is serious," she said. "He just shrugs, no matter what I say. He doesn't care about anything, and it's really annoying."

Zita walked, deep in thought. A furrow appeared on his brow. "It sounds like serious depression," he said. "Maybe he should get treatment. Maybe there are some pills that could help him get out of it."

Carmen shook her head. "You won't get Nicolai to take pills," she said. "He's totally against them. Let's take the path, even though it's slightly longer. When we get home again, he's bound to be there. And sorry to say it, but screw him."

Zita made no comment to this. And they walked on in silence.

"We'll be getting the puppy in three weeks," she said enthusiastically. "I'm really looking forward to it."

"And Nicolai?" Zita asked. "Is he indifferent about the puppy as well?"

"Yes, he couldn't care less about anything. But I'm sure he'll fall in love with it, like me. There's just something about puppies."

She fell silent again. She had to work hard to keep up. Her father had long legs and kept a steady pace. It took them twenty minutes to walk to Stranda, but there was no Nicolai to be seen by the water. The waves rolled in lazily and broke along the shore. Carmen strained her eyes, staring out onto the horizon. Zita wandered along the water, picked up a stick, and then threw it down again almost immediately.

"Do you remember when you were little?" he started. "Do you remember all the good times we had, you and I?"

"Yes, of course. You used to carry me on your shoulders," Carmen said.

Then she dried a tear and looked at him with her worried blue eyes.

"What if he's not back by this evening?" she said. "What if it gets dark? What will we do then?"

When they got back, Pappa Zita went straight to the bedroom, as if he thought that Nicolai had come home and gone to bed in a moment of desperate loneliness. It was of course a possibility, and he did not want to imagine the worst. But the room was empty and quiet, just the bed with two crumpled comforters. Carmen sat down by the kitchen table, exhausted and confused.

"Have you been down to the cellar?" he asked tentatively.

Her answer was swift, with a slight sigh: "No, but I shouted down to him, obviously. From the top of the stairs, I mean, just in case. And he didn't answer, so he must be out. I'm fairly sure he must be. Don't talk like that," she added hastily, "it makes me nervous."

They sat for a while looking at each other, and Zita's eyes were narrow with doubt and uncertainty. He picked up the saltshaker that was on the table, unscrewed the top, and then put it back on again. His hands suddenly looked so big and out of proportion on the scrubbed table, with nothing to hold.

"I'll go down and have a look," he said, "just to make sure. You sit here and wait; I'll be back in a minute."

Carmen nodded but didn't say anything. Her father got up and went into the hall. She heard his feet on the stairs, clearly at first, but then more and more muffled as he descended into the dim cellar. A minute ticked by, and her thoughts started to wander to darker places. She couldn't help it. More than anything she wanted to get up and go out into the hall and shout down to him and ask if everything was all right. But she couldn't move. Dad, she thought, you have to find him. Well and alive. You have to sort this out, like you always do. Because this is more than I can stand. Two minutes passed and the silence was deafening. Once again she heard the humming in the air, but this time it got louder. She looked nervously out of the window, staring down at the horrible dark pond. What if he'd drowned himself? What if the worst thing imaginable had happened? She had experienced so much tragedy in her short life. No, she reprimanded herself. He's just fixing the bikes. They'll come into the kitchen at any moment, and Nicolai will be happy and smiling. He'll be smiling because he's pulled through, she thought. Life will be the same again, all smiles and laughter. And they could walk hand in hand out into the big wide world, happy as skylarks.

"Carmen," he said in anguish.

His arms were hanging loose by his sides and his eyes were black.

"Carmen, you're going to have to be strong. Nicolai has hanged himself in the cellar. Presumably last night while you were asleep. Don't go down. Stay up here and wait. I'll call for help."

"It's not my fault," she screamed. "It's not my fault!" She tipped down toward the floor, taking the chair with her as she fell. She tried to get to her feet again but was weak and frail. He scooped her up in his strong arms.

"Sit down!" he ordered, pushing her into a chair. "Sit still and don't move!"

She collapsed onto the table and cried with shock and pain.

Pappa Zita went downstairs into the basement for the second time. Thirteen heavy steps in a somber spiral. This time he had a lump in his throat and a knife he had found in the kitchen drawer. He registered the open toolbox, oilcan, and overalls on the floor. Two old bikes had fallen over. And of course there was a good deal of junk, like the box of old schoolbooks. The sight of Nicolai hanging from the rafter was so shocking that he gasped. A plastic garden chair lay upended beneath the primitive gallows. He righted the chair and stood on it. He put one arm around the thin boy's body and cut the rope. The body fell to the floor with a dull thud. He got down from the chair and pulled his cell phone out of his pocket, intending to dial 911. His fingers were shaking so much that he got it wrong again and again, but finally he heard a voice at the other end. He explained the situation and then remained sitting in the chair, trying to gather his thoughts.

It was while he sat there that he spotted Tommy's crib in the corner. It had been taken apart, and the mattress was lying beside it. He was filled with sudden unease when he saw this. And he remembered what Nicolai had said down on the jetty the day after Tommy had died.

There's a lot you don't know.

Now he wondered what he had meant by those words, and a hint of fear knotted in his stomach. But the thoughts that filled his mind were so awful that he pushed them to one side. He refused to think them. He had to believe his daughter's distraught explanation; anything else would be impossible to bear. And yet he was extremely shaken by seeing the crib. There's a lot you don't know. There's a lot you don't know. It went around and around in his head, like a scratched record he couldn't stop. Eventually he went back upstairs to Carmen. He picked her up from the chair and hugged her tight, all the while tormented by the difficult questions he didn't dare to ask. In the end, he mustered the courage. He put her back down into the chair and looked her in the eye.

"His crib," he whispered. "Tommy's crib. It's down in the cellar. What were you thinking? It's damp down there, and the mattress will be ruined. It'll get moldy, Carmen, you know that?" Carmen immediately started to cry and threw her arms around him, sobbing uncontrollably.

"No," she stammered. "I didn't want the memories. I couldn't bear to see the empty bed. And if we have another baby, we'll get new stuff."

Zita comforted himself that this was understandable. There was a wisp of fear there that he could not ignore, but it was not the time for confrontation. He took Carmen with him into the living room and they sat on the sofa. He put his arm around her shoulders, trying to console her.

"Don't be angry," he said quietly. "Don't carry this with you through life as rage. Then you'll never get over it. You have to forgive."

Soon they heard the cars. Only a few minutes had passed, and they both went out onto the front step to meet them. They recognized Jacob Skarre standing beside the police car.

"I've already cut him down; he's lying on the floor in the cellar," Zita said. "We don't know when it happened. He drove off last night around eleven o'clock and must have come back from his night drive at some point. It all happened while Carmen was asleep."

She stayed in the living room when they carried Nicolai's body up from the cellar, strapped onto a narrow stretcher. She followed the police's advice and didn't look at him. They said it was a terrible sight. Her father had told her in a firm voice that she did not want to carry the image with her; she had to remember Nicolai as he was. So she kept out of the way, even though she was aching with curiosity. In a strange way, the drama turned her on. But there was something in her father's face, something ominous that she took seriously. Skarre came into the living room with all his questions. How had yesterday been, if he had shown any signs, if she had found any letters, if she had suspected that something was up. If he had a history of depression, if there had been other suicides in the family. No, he was just the same as always, Carmen said. I'm in shock.

Skarre went on for an hour, digging and asking questions. He wanted to know everything. He wandered around the house as though he was looking for evidence. What kind of evidence, she wondered in desperation. There's nothing to find. What had happened was Nicolai's final wish, and she couldn't understand it. He had been willing to die, to put a noose around his neck and jump. Alone in the dark cellar. When he could have been lying safely in a warm bed, with her hand in his. The thought of it made her cold as ice. And she told Skarre the truth, that he'd left the house around eleven the night before and driven off in the Golf. He told her that he just wanted to go for a drive and stroked her cheek. For the last time. But how was she to know, she thought. She was used to him driving off; he was a loner. But now she remembered everything in detail. His breath on her face, the slim, warm hand on her cheek, the clear green eyes. His footsteps on the ground as he walked to the car, the engine starting. The red taillights disappearing around the dark bend.

Afterward, when they had left and taken the body with them, she went to Møllergata 4 with her father. She could scarcely walk on her own through the door. Everything felt cold and unreal and incomprehensible. She lay in her parents' bed, flat on her back, without moving. And while she waited to feel like herself again, she watched a fly buzzing around the ceiling light. Her lower back ached, but she couldn't be bothered to change position. She lay there as though dead. She could lie like that forever, without moving, watching the fly. It buzzed around energetically, furry, black, and revolting. Zita came into the room and sat down on the edge of the bed. He grasped her hand and squeezed tight.

"You'll stay here with us," he said.

She didn't answer, because she had nothing to say. She had no drive or willpower left. She wanted to get up, but something was holding her down. It felt like a wall. She knew that time was passing and that outside the door life went on. It was almost impossible to understand that people could laugh and joke. But it carried on, regardless, irrepressible life. Her father went back to Granfoss to pick up some clothes and her medicine. She asked him to bring her diary back too. It was at the back of the bottom drawer in the desk.

"Is it helpful?"

"Yes," she said, "I write in it every day. It's like everything is easier when I can write about it."

She tried to sleep but couldn't. She just lay there in bed and stared blankly. She wanted to get up and engage but felt that she was expected to lie there. At least for the first devastating twenty-four hours. She opened and closed her hands, as if she wanted to help the blood pump around her body. The fly didn't stop; it was so caught up in its busy little life. A few longer spins around the room, but always back to the light in the eternal pursuit of light and warmth. Just like people.

36

DEAR DIARY,

Today is the worst day ever. And I am writing to you in sorrow and desperation. Because Nicolai has hanged himself in the cellar, and the shock triggered a major epileptic seizure. It's not strange at all that I finally collapsed. Dad has been sitting by my bed and I've been lying here ever since. The sustained cramps have left me exhausted. When I woke up and came to, I'd forgotten everything. Dad had to tell me the whole tragic story all over again. That Nicolai had gotten up on a chair and then thrown himself off. Is that cowardly or courageous? I don't know. All I know is that now I am bitterly sad and disappointed that he left me. And angry. And one thing holds true and that is that I'm strong and resilient. No one will ever send me over the edge.

So I finally came around. And the fly that had been buzzing by the light had disappeared. Maybe it had found a crack in the wood somewhere in the bedroom where it could die a quiet death. It's autumn, after all. It's so strange that I remembered that detail but had actually forgotten that Nicolai was dead.

I know that I foam at the mouth when I have a fit. And sometimes I wet myself, which is just hideous. Of all the things that come with my condition, that embarrasses me the most. But Dad is tactful. Because obviously I'm proud and I worry about my appearance. But I've lived with this for so long that I guess I don't care anymore. Right now, though, it's too much, I've had enough.

Still, I'm lying here and I'm alive. Now I can start all over again. Everything is open in the years ahead, and I want to see this as a new chapter. After all, like the Chinese say, a crisis is a new opportunity, isn't it? And outside the window the moon is still shining white. It's hard to imagine that they've been up there with a rocket. I've tried to understand it, and I can to a point. At least you can see the moon. You just need to head straight for it, that shining white disc in the dark sky. But when it comes to Mars, I'm lost. Because you can't see Mars, it's so far away. How did they manage to get there? They just fired the engine. It makes me realize that people have endless potential. So I must be able to succeed in a few things. A new man, a new baby, a new life. And Dad will keep me going. Mom has made me some hot milk and honey. As if that would ease the pain. But I do what they say. I drink the hot milk and cry on Dad's shoulder. Nicolai is dead. And no matter what they say, I have to see him with my own eyes to believe it.

37

TWELFTH OF OCTOBER. Morning.

What sad times, he thought. The leaves are falling from the trees and rotting on the ground. Nature is freezing over and Nicolai is dead. As a rule, he only met his own eyes fleetingly when he looked in the mirror. There was an odd shyness; even though he was handsome, it didn't make much difference. But now, today, the twelfth, he stood and studied himself with renewed interest. He stared at himself, searching for signs of weakness. And he certainly found them. The lines by the corners of his mouth were more marked. But how could I have prevented it, he asked himself. When someone has decided on it, it's not easy to prevent death; it's not easy to stop them falling out of time. And yet he was weighed down by sorrow at Nicolai's death. No way back, once you're hanging from the noose. A strong nylon rope was enough. But now perhaps he was reunited with Tommy, even though he didn't believe that either. Death was cold and final, the cessation of life and nothing else.

When he had finished shaving, which he did with extra care given the day's plans, he went out into the kitchen. He put on the coffee and buttered a piece of bread. Frank padded over to his water bowl for a drink, knowing that he would get his morning walk if he was patient. Following this simple breakfast, Sejer went into the hall and clipped on the leash. Together they walked down the stairs and came out into the parking lot. The morning sky was gray with mist and it was drizzling. There's nearly always guilt, in some form or other, attached to death, he thought. There was always something you could have done differently and better. Carmen would now be feeling guilty, as was Marian Zita. Just like I'm feeling guilty, he thought. He pulled at the leash, struggling to get the dog to follow him. Something had been there before them, a bitch perhaps. Now it was too late and Nicolai's death tormented him. But his thoughts drifted on to other things. Frank had found a pinecone. He carried it proudly in his mouth and lifted his leg as dogs are wont to do. A quarter of an hour later, he turned and walked back to the apartment.

Well, he thought when he had driven into the center, I'm about to get my final verdict now. No matter what, he'd take it like a man, even if it was perhaps terminal. He had always been balanced by nature: patient, calm, and rational. No one lived forever. He parked the car and went into the medical practice. There were others waiting. He dutifully took a pair of blue shoe covers from the basket and put them on. They looked ridiculous and none of the others in the waiting room had done the same.

While he waited, he read a medical journal. He believed that his health was generally very good, even though he was prone to melancholy and was a worrier by nature. He had managed well in life so far. Through the grief and loss of Elise, through unrelenting murder cases. Yes, he had been strong and stubborn and robust all his life. Dedicated and almost self-sacrificing in relation to the people he served. And here he was reading about five-year-old American children on antidepressants and toddlers taking sleeping pills, incredible. He himself had never taken anything other than acetaminophen, on the rare occasion that he got a headache.

But there was nothing that helped for dizziness, other than keeping as still as possible until it passed.

He waited for nearly an hour, his body restless and on edge. Finally a nurse came to the door and called his name. The plastic shoe covers rustled as he walked across the scrubbed floor.

The doctor was alarmingly young, but Sejer felt he was given the best care. He was asked how long he had had this dizziness that came and went, which so often threw him off balance and to the floor. When he answered, he was embarrassed and awkward.

"I'd rather not answer that," he said. "Not without my lawyer here."

The doctor, Hannah Chen, smiled with white teeth and looked at him indulgently. "I see," she said. "I take it that it's been some time since your last visit. You're certainly not part of the furniture here."

"I'm sorry; I never make an appointment unless it's urgent," he said. "I'm a cautious man."

She referred him to Oslo University Hospital for an MRI, and he realized there was no getting away from it; the bugger was going to be caught once and for all. Then she started to ask him about all kinds of things, and he answered as best he could. No, there's no history of cancer in my family. My father had a bad heart, and my mother died of kidney failure; she was born with only one kidney and then it got inflamed. Both of them lived to a good age though. My wife died of liver cancer, some years ago now. She was only forty. No, I don't drink much. Just a whiskey in the evening. Although, to be honest, it's quite a generous dram. And I smoke one single cigarette every day and have for years. But I believe in moderation. Otherwise I lead a healthy life. My diet is rather Spartan; I keep fit. I'm never ill. Never. This is a new experience in my very orderly life, whatever it is that's bothering me.

And yes, I'm a bit anxious. So what do you think? Will I live until Christmas?

Dr. Chen made some short notes. Her black hair was swept up into a tight, shiny bun on the top of her head.

"I'm guessing you will," she said calmly. "But we have to take this seriously. You're not getting any younger, I'm sorry to say. None of us are. The human body is an intricate thing, and it's amazing that so many manage to get by without mishap well into old age. People have never lived as long as we do now. And you'll live to be old too, just you wait and see. So, I'm going to ask you to go to the lab and get some blood tests, and then you can go home safe in the knowledge that things have been set in motion. The hospital will send you a letter about your appointment. Try not to worry. You really are in very good shape."

He tried to calm his nerves and push the thoughts from his mind. In the afternoon, he drove over to Pappa Zita's house. Carmen opened the door, came onto the front step, and held out her hand with a brave smile. She said nothing at first, as if she had gotten stuck, but then she composed herself and managed to speak.

"Oh, have you come to bother us again?" she said with a dark, defiant flash.

She walked into the hall and then closed the door behind him with a slam.

"No," Sejer replied. "I haven't come to bother you. I just wanted to give my condolences, because this is all so terribly sad. I feel it too. And you have experienced more tragedy than anyone deserves. That was all I wanted to say, that my thoughts are with you."

"It would be nice if you came to the funeral," she said. "Because he liked you a lot. He said so. Dad isn't at home. He had to go to Zita Quick for a meeting. The business is growing, so we have to employ more people. I'm going to start working again soon, because I've been at home for so long now. You can bring the dog in if he's out in the car. But to be honest, I think it's time you left me alone now."

The words just poured out. It was as if she feared silence, because it would reveal something. Because when nothing is said, your body can betray you with a thousand small signals—nervous hands, a twitch of the mouth—even though she was doing all she could to be relaxed. He declined the offer and said that Frank was fine in the car; he was used to waiting. Was she not going to talk about Nicolai? How could she ignore his death? He couldn't understand what she was thinking.

"Is it true that they break their neck?" she asked, suddenly looking at him directly. "Is it quick?"

He looked her in the eye and thought for a moment before answering.

"Yes, that's right," he said, almost reluctantly. "And yes, so you know, it is quick. It takes about five to ten seconds before they fall into a coma."

She sat for a while thinking, digesting the information.

"But those seconds must be awful. Everything twisting. All that blood left in the head."

"Yes," he said. "Possibly. But we'll never know, will we?"

"Do they go blue in the face? Do their tongues stick out of their mouths?"

"I haven't seen Nicolai, so I can't tell you."

"Or you don't want to," she said curtly. "You want to protect me. Well, that's fine by me. But if I want to see him, then no one can stop me. And if I want you to leave me alone, then you'll leave me alone."

"Of course," he said, "but think hard before you do it. The image will haunt you for a long time to come. And the beautiful picture you have of Nicolai might be lost forever. Think about it before you sacrifice those happy memories. Where is your mother today? Are you alone?"

"Mom's gone out," she said. "But she'll be back in an hour. Would you like me to make some coffee? Just say if you want some, and I'll get it."

Again, he declined the offer, observing her intently all the while. She was wearing a flowery top and three-quarter-length pants, and looked very pretty with her platinum hair and big eyes. All her life she had bathed in others' admiration, looking in the mirror and admiring herself. It was as though she was always posing. He didn't care much for it, but it was an attitude he had noticed with other girls too.

"This must be more than you can bear," he said in a friendly voice. He struggled to overcome the edge of antipathy that he always felt in his meetings with Carmen.

"Yes, it's enough now. But I want to find a new boyfriend. That's if there's anyone who wants me."

She cocked her head when she said this. The statement caught him off guard. Was that really what she was thinking, a day after Nicolai had committed suicide: a new man?

"Carmen, really," he said, smiling. "I don't think you need to worry about things like that now."

She smiled back. "Good, that's all I wanted to hear," she clucked. Then they both laughed a short burst of liberating laughter, despite all the sadness.

"Will you be using the same funeral directors?"

"Yes, we've got an appointment with them this evening. They're coming around at seven. We've told them what happened; it was Dad who told them. You know what, they took it well, because they have to. We're going to tell the truth in the church, that it was suicide. I'm sure that's what Nicolai would have wanted. He didn't like sweeping things under the rug. You might not know it, but I really did love him."

"I believe you," Sejer said. Then he asked: "Did you notice anything in the days before? When he left the house yesterday evening?"

"I've known there was something wrong ever since Tommy died," she said. "He's not been himself since. He was really down in Majorca, didn't care about anything. Just moped around, chain-smoked, and drank whiskey. I couldn't get through to him. So I was very worried. But I wasn't that surprised really. Nicolai is very reserved and always has been. And I often worried what he might do."

"Do you know where he went yesterday?"

"No, I've got no idea. I suppose he just drove around in the Golf. He might have gone down to Stranda. I went to bed about midnight and fell asleep right away. When I realized that he hadn't slept in the bed, I got really worried. I'm so glad that it was Dad who found him, so at least I didn't get the worst shock."

She picked at the scuffed pink nail polish on one of her nails.

"He didn't go to Stranda," Sejer told her. "He came to see me. I found him on the stairs around midnight."

"What?" She opened her eyes wide.

"He came to tell me something important; it wasn't a long visit."

"Something important?" she repeated and looked confused. "What was it?"

"I can't tell you. But I'm taking it very seriously."

"But what did you talk about?"

"Well, he was worried about the court case. And then we talked a bit about you and your last statement."

She pouted, as though she was sulking. "Yes, Nicolai was furious that I told the truth. But that's always best, isn't it?"

"Yes, I agree. So, Carmen, how will your life be without Nicolai?"

"Well, I'll just have to make it work, won't I? And Dad will do everything he can to help me."

"And how is your epilepsy? Are you managing to control it?"

"Oh yes," she said. "It'll always be there. But I've just had a major seizure, so at least I know it'll be some time until the next one. But generally, it's OK as long as I remember to take my pills. Dad keeps an eye on me, because I sometimes forget. And by the way, it's Mom who tends Tommy's grave. She thinks it's better for me not to go. She's planted some ivy and it's growing nicely."

"I know," Sejer said. "I've been up there. And you've got Friis as your lawyer," he added. "He'll look after you well; he's good. Be honest with him and he'll do all he can to help you."

"He says that I should be cleared," she said, "because everything that's happened is so terrible. Because I was mentally incapacitated. After the epileptic fit I wasn't thinking straight. I thought I had to cover it up. He's already spoken to my physician. And I'm not worried about the case; I'm going to manage it. Say hello to Skarre for me. He's nice but he does go on a bit."

He promised he would and asked her to take care of herself. Then he got up from the sofa and walked toward the door. She followed him and then grabbed his arm and grasped it as tight as she could.

"I'm going to tell you something," she said, "something you might not know."

"OK."

He continued into the hall and started to open the front door.

"Over sixty percent of fetuses with Down syndrome are aborted; they're never born. People don't want to have them."

He stopped and looked her in the eye. He was rather horrified by the statement; six out of ten Down children, he thought—was that really true? And he wondered what people with Down syndrome thought of the statistic. That they shouldn't be here at all, that lots of people wouldn't want them, that they were a burden?

"Why are you telling me that?" he asked as he opened the door.

"I just wanted you to know," she said. "And I think I deserve sympathy, because no one understands how hard it is to have a child like that."

He went out onto the step and turned and put his hand on her arm.

"Yes," he said with a smile. "You have all my sympathy. But no one gets what they deserve in this life. Please take good care of yourself. And no matter what you might think, I wish you well." Then he said goodbye and went to his car. He saw her still standing on the step as he drove away.

38

NINETEENTH OF OCTOBER. Rain.

The sky was dark and threatening on the day Nicolai was laid to rest in Møller Church, and they had to battle pelting rain, wind, and fog. Trees and bushes, flags and sails were tossed around as the rain bucketed down. A modest gathering of neighbors and friends, colleagues from Zita Quick, and uncles from Barcelona followed him to the grave, which lay beside Tommy's under the birch trees. As they came out of the church and were about to walk down the stone path to the gaping grave, the rain intensified. But the priest remained unperturbed, even though the wind tore angrily at his vestments, revealing his spindly legs and worn-out shoes. He continued on determinedly toward his destination as was expected of him, his neck bowed in humble prayer. Carmen sought shelter behind her father's broad back and sang the last psalm as best she could. *"Abide with me, fast falls the eventide."*

"Ashes to ashes, dust to dust," the priest chanted as he threw three shovels of dry dirt on the white coffin lid. Nothing had been arranged for after the funeral this time either. In the death notice, it had said that the funeral would finish at the grave. Carmen just wanted it over and done with. Her mouth trembled as she clung to her father like an exhausted child. In part out of a sense of loss, but most of all out of panic. Because her life was out of control.

"Must be a message from above," Skarre commented when the ceremony was over and they hurried back to the Volvo to seek shelter from the rain. "It's been the driest and warmest autumn in memory. But today there's a downpour."

"What did you think of the priest?" Sejer asked. "Did he pass?"

Skarre closed the car door and dried the rain from his face.

"The priest was excellent," he said. "A pillar of strength. Nicolai would have liked him. No avoidance or vague explanations, just the truth, and that's the way it should be. Not even the pouring rain put him off his stride. To be honest, the stormy weather seemed quite appropriate today. What about you?" he added. "Do you feel guilty?"

"Yes," Sejer replied. "I should have heard the alarm bells; I should have heard them and done something."

He put a Fisherman's Friend in his mouth and ran his fingers through his wet, coarse hair.

"He said it outright, that he wouldn't be present at the court hearing. Then he left the apartment and went straight to the everafter. I'll never forgive myself."

He stared glumly at his younger colleague. His eyes pleaded with Skarre for understanding.

"Console yourself with the fact that you would only have managed to delay it for a while," he said in a comforting tone. "It would only have happened later. I believe that suicide is like a ticking bomb in the genes. Sooner or later it will explode and nothing in the world can stop it."

"Thank you for that. I'll still always feel guilty, though. But I'll just have to live with that."

"Everyone lives with guilt," Skarre stated. "Welcome to the club."

"Well, you'll have to file a complaint with God," Sejer commented.

"Come on, God can't be responsible for everything. We humans have to take some responsibility too."

"But isn't He the almighty? Isn't that the point of it all?"

"Yes," Skarre conceded. "But I could talk forever about His inscrutable ways. I'm pretty unflappable, and you will never make me lose hope. The explanation will come," he claimed.

"On the Day of Judgment, you mean?"

"Yes, why not? And you know, there's an explanation for everything we wonder about, for all the mysteries. There is an answer. Does God exist or doesn't He? Is there life after death or not? Everything can be answered with a simple yes or no. Imagine."

"Good of you to simplify things," Sejer said, "but I just can't bring myself to believe it. We'll never get those answers. When did you become so sure of God's existence?"

"Oh, I've never been certain," Skarre quickly assured him.

"But you said you believed?"

"I believe, but I don't know; that's something different. It would be easier, of course, if I experienced a miracle. It wouldn't need to be a big one. But I've never really been the type for absolute certainty. And anyway, doubt makes us human."

Sejer didn't sleep well that night.

He tossed and turned, pushing the comforter away because he was too hot and pulling it up again because he got too cold. He kept changing positions and could not settle. And finally with the first light he sank into the restless world of dreams. He dreamed that he was running for his life through dry sand. Behind him, his pursuer had a gun; he could make out a figure in black with a hood and flapping coattails. He could clearly hear him breathing, and every now and then the man gave a kind of low, terrifying growl that scared the living daylights out of him. When he turned around to see who it was, he discovered that the white face beneath the hood was not a human face but a clock face, and that the hands were pointing to twelve. He kicked up clouds of sand in panic. But instead of moving forward, he just dug himself deeper and deeper into the sand dunes. A bullet would hit him at any second, through the left-hand side of his back, shredding his heart. Blood would flow and death would be upon him. But despite the panic, somewhere deep inside there was a rumble that this was perhaps just a dream and nothing to worry about. Still he scrambled to get away. Fascinating, all the layers between being awake and deep sleep, he mused once awake. Feeling agitated and tired, he leaned over the edge of the bed and looked down at Frank.

"That was a bad dream," he said and groaned. Frank opened his eyes, stood up, and trotted to the head of the bed. He got a rub behind the ear and then went and lay down again. Sejer fell back to sleep, only to dream the same dream again. The feeling of kicking helplessly in the dry sand without being able to move made him panic. Later, when he woke up for the second time, he wondered what the dream might mean. There was something fateful about it, he thought, because the clock hands showed twelve. That meant that time was out—could that be it? Was his subconscious trying to tell him there was no hope? That the dizziness was his final fate? He tossed the comforter to one side and put his feet on the floor. I guess I'm ill, he thought disconsolately, and felt a sharp pain in his chest. And yes, it was the left side. Could there be something wrong with his heart? he wondered. Was his life about to collapse? He went over to the window and looked out at the town blanketed in darkness. And he was struck by a melancholy thought. He would never know the answers to life's great questions, and God would never reveal Himself to him. But we're modest, aren't we? he said to Frank. I would be happy with a burning bush.

39

WHEN THE DAY finally came that Dr. Chen called him with the MRI results, he was on his way back to the car after a short trip into the town center. His senses were so clear that day, as if everything was for the last time. November with its bare branches and soft drizzle, the smell of wet leaves, heavy leaden clouds, birds migrating south in great skeins across the gray sky. He noticed an Opel with dirty windows, an old man in an electric wheelchair whirring along the pavement, a teenager on a bike. He saw all these things with crystal clarity. He sprinted back to the car, let Frank into the back, and then settled in the driver's seat. He put the phone to his ear, aware of his accelerating heartbeat.

"We've found something," Dr. Chen said. "Are you sitting down?"

The words vibrated in the air. Her voice was remarkably neutral, which immediately made him nervous. That's not what you were supposed to say, he thought. You were supposed to say everything is fine, that I'm perfectly healthy and that life will go on. You were supposed to say it was nothing more than a misunderstanding, and that it is all over now. That I can breathe out again.

"What kind of something?" he asked in a thin voice. He, the

detective inspector who normally spoke in a clear bass, was whispering like a girl.

"Acusticus neurinoma," Chen replied. As if the diagnosis was the most natural thing in the world.

"I see," he said, "but I'm afraid I don't speak Latin. What is that in everyday language?"

"I know," she apologized. "I was just quoting from the letter from the hospital. An acoustic tumor is a benign tumor and is generally located in the inner ear. It presses against the vestibular, or balance nerve, which is why you get so dizzy. Have you noticed any hearing loss?"

He had to think for a moment. Yes, maybe, a little in the right ear, but his anxiety about the dizziness had overshadowed it.

"A tumor," he hesitated. "That doesn't sound good."

"No, no, everything should be fine," Chen reassured him. "It is in all likelihood benign. But it won't be smooth sailing. You see, it's not going to be easy to remove it as it's in the inner ear, which is very delicate. In other words, it's hard to get to it."

"Do I have to have an operation?" he asked in alarm.

The electric wheelchair was approaching his car. The old man didn't even bother to look at him; he was obviously on an urgent mission.

"Yes, you will have to have an operation—if you don't want to go through life with your head spinning like a drunkard, that is," she explained. "It is absolutely possible to remove it. In fact, there are several different ways in which it can be done. But it is a complex operation, so it's not easy. The surgeon will have to decide which method is best for you, so I'll get back to you."

"But tell me one thing," he said feebly. "Will I need an anesthetic?"

"My dear man," Chen said with a laugh, "we're not living in

203

the Middle Ages. Of course you'll be under general anesthetic, so don't you worry."

He thought about it and tried to calm himself. He looked at Frank in the mirror; he was lying peacefully with his head on his paws, blissfully unaware of how serious this was. You superficial little mutt, he mumbled to himself, as he held the cell phone tight in his sweaty hand.

"We could use what is called a gamma knife," Chen continued. "In which case, we go in through the auditory canal and remove the tumor from there. It is the cleanest method, if you like. Then there is another more invasive method where we go in just under the temporal bone using a scalpel and remove it from there. Both methods are very successful, so we just need to determine which is best for you. We often leave the tumors where they are, believe it or not. But as it is bothering you, we must do something; don't you agree? I'm afraid you will have to be prepared to be added to the waiting list. The system works well, but it is often slow."

She paused. He could hear her breathing, fast and easy. The electric wheelchair had now cleared the car and the old man whirred on, eyes straight ahead on his steady course. The windshield was covered in small drops of condensation.

"But you must be a busy man, Detective Inspector, so I will try to bump you up the list," she said.

The relief flooded through him, making him feel warm and light. I've got a few years left, he thought, how wonderful!

"So I'll be hearing from the hospital then?"

"Yes, you'll get a letter. And otherwise, you're fit as a fiddle. All the tests were good. And there is no doubt that you will be living on this earth for a while yet."

Then she said goodbye and he sat quietly in the car for some time. He couldn't seem to get moving again. His pulse was back to normal and his breathing was slow and steady. Benign, she'd said, benign. What a relief! More left of life, after all. It was almost too good to be true. Then thoughts started to crowd his mind once again, just as the old man in the wheelchair disappeared around the corner. A cure was within reach. But first, they would have to stick a knife in his ear.

40

THE COLD WEATHER arrived finally in December, with heavy frosts.

The puddles had a top layer of paper-thin ice in the morning, the grass stood like pins, and hoarfrost covered the bare silver branches. Tommy, Carmen, and Nicolai slipped in and out of his mind. The case was due to be heard on June 24, but new cases took priority. Because people never stopped; they flared up at the slightest offense. They shot each other with guns and stabbed each other with knives. Then they said that they hadn't meant to. I didn't want this to happen, he provoked me, fell onto the knife, it was him or me. In all honesty, it was self-defense. I plead not guilty, because it was all a terrible accident, and I deeply regret it. A couple of thousand people disappeared or were reported missing every year, but most of them turned up again safe and sound. They often gave vague explanations of where they had been and what they had done. Thousands of convicted criminals evaded prison, failed to return from prison leave, or simply went on the run before being convicted. Some were found floating in swimming pools, others under a tree in the woods. Always, he mused, almost always under a tree. And the circumstances were not necessarily suspicious. Many had made the same choice as Nicolai. A fast and dramatic exit from time.

He had his operation on January 20.

It took place at eight o'clock in the morning at Oslo University Hospital, and he was more nervous than he liked to admit. His heart was racing as they wheeled him into the operating room, ten milligrams of Valium having no apparent effect. He was a big man. The white light on the ceiling blinded him, so he closed his eyes. He said a silent prayer, and then immediately felt ashamed. He didn't believe in anything, certainly not a higher power. But now he had no other comfort than his pathetic prayer. Let everything go well; help me get through this. And a wretched, embarrassed amen.

They had decided to use the gamma knife and he was grateful for it. When he came to, the first thing he felt was immense relief that it was all over. He had struggled with the dizziness for so long, and now his head felt clear and light. He was allowed to go home right away. Ingrid came to collect him and they went back to her house for something to eat. Frank was waiting there, and he was overjoyed to see him.

"Next time there's something wrong, don't wait so long," Ingrid reprimanded him. "You're impossible."

He raised his hand and promised.

41

DETECTIVE CHIEF SUPERINTENDENT Holthemann retired at the age of fifty-eight. He was not the sort of person who made friends and was not particularly good with people, but he was an extremely skilled administrator and was well respected in Søndre Buskerud Police District. He always managed to meet his budgets and the ranks were well disciplined from the top down. Despite Holthemann's cantankerous nature, Sejer knew that he would miss the sound of his stick in the narrow, busy corridors and his reprimanding bass and piercing eyes. People pooled together to buy a cake. As if retirement was something to celebrate. Holthemann didn't know what to think, what it all meant, now that it was over. But he certainly stepped down from his important position with high blood sugar. Skarre aspired to carry on Holthemann's legacy, despite his young age, and even Sejer had been asked to apply for the position. But he wasn't tempted by administration; he wanted to be out in the field. He had always wanted to be close to tragedy, in the front row of life's drama, where he met people. And when it came to Carmen Zita, he still questioned what had happened. But he had gotten nowhere with the young mother. She was strong, proud, and stubborn, and she had kept repeating her story of a seizure and the ensuing confusion.

It was as if he was wading through heavy snow. It was hard

work and progress was slow. He thought about what Nicolai had once said, that Carmen was like a piano string and would never break. We'll see, he mused. Everyone has a breaking point, even you, little Miss Carmen; I won't give up. And so time passed, week by week, with periods of intense cold and heavy snowfall. Freezing cold black nights and blinding white days. Glittering sun and drifting snow: a pitiless winter. In March, the sun began to melt the snow and slowly but surely it trickled away and spring made an appearance. He thought of the promise he had made to himself that he would fight for justice, that somehow or other he would dig out the truth. But deep down, he had no idea how he would do it. It tormented him day and night for long periods. There was not a shred of evidence, just an elaborate story. The beautiful owned the world, he thought despondently, and everyone would be taken in by Carmen's tears. She would win, because that was how she was. She was like the scorpion; she would get across the river alive.

42

HE DID NOT see her again until early summer. He first noticed her as he walked across the square and could not believe his eyes. He stood there staring with a smile on his lips. Because Carmen Zita really was a sight to behold as she walked between the market stalls in the cobbled square. He managed to pull himself together and went over to say hello, but could not hide his surprise as she stood there blooming in front of him. A Jack Russell danced at her feet.

"Well, well, well," he said, astounded. "Things have obviously moved on since I saw you last. What wonderful news; when is the baby due?"

She laughed and patted her small, round belly, which was noticeable as she was otherwise so slim.

"Four months," she said. "I'm past the first trimester."

She laughed again, unashamedly happy.

"I've had amnio and the baby's fine," she told him. "I'm so lucky."

Sejer thought about Tommy, who had not met Carmen's expectations, with a heavy heart. He understood her anxiety and that she needed reassurance; of course he did. Many would have done the same, he admitted. Elise and I would have done the same, because that's how people are. That's life—everyone wants perfection, everyone wants a child without disabilities or deformities.

"And who is the lucky father?" he asked. He wanted to be friendly, because nothing was certain in terms of the hearing. And he had to accept the court's ruling no matter what, and any doubt was very definitely in Carmen Zita's favor. He knew all this, but still it bothered him, because sometimes the system failed.

"His name's Anders," Carmen said with a smile. "He's not particularly happy about it. He says that it's all a bit too fast; but, well, it's happened. And anyway, it doesn't matter if Anders is worried about it," she said cheerily, "because I'm not. If there's something I'm good at, it's being a mom."

Quite, Sejer said to himself. Then he thought about Anders, who wasn't particularly happy about becoming a father. It wasn't the best start in life for a new baby, but she didn't care about that. She really was quite a force to be reckoned with, so full of hope and optimism. He'd seldom seen the like. And maybe the child would grow up and have a good life; it was absolutely a possibility. What do I know? he deliberated. I don't hold the truth about people and life.

"Your case is coming up on the twenty-fourth," he said in a kind voice. "How do you feel about it, Carmen? Are you dreading the final judgment?"

"No, what have I got to worry about?" she twittered like a lark. "I can only tell the truth, and the truth always wins in the end. Isn't that what they say? And you know, sometimes it hurts, but that really is the only way. Friis is very optimistic. He says that everything will be fine, and I trust him. And being pregnant will help as well. The judge will have more sympathy for someone who's going to be a mother. They can't lock me up, because I have to look after the baby. Because no one else can take my place. It's my job. And I won't run away from my responsibility. I'm going to do this," she said with determination and force. She tugged at her lovely dress and looked very pleased with herself. The Jack Russell sniffed around Sejer's shoes. It was a short-haired brown, white, and black terrier: small, energetic, and neat.

Yes, Sejer thought, disheartened. The jury will believe your story, I'm sure. Carmen Zita from Granfoss was obviously not a hardened criminal. She was a young, whimsical girl he would never understand. It annoyed him intensely that the truth might always remain a secret. He patted the little dog on the head.

"Well, I guess I'll see you in court then," he said with a smile. "And no matter what you might think, Carmen, I wish you well."

"Thank you," she said. "That's kind of you. We're friends now, aren't we? Tell Jacob Skarre I've forgiven him all the stress."

"Yes, of course we're friends," he said. "You take good care of yourself and the baby. See you in court."

Then she carried on across the big market square and disappeared between the stalls. With a growing baby in her belly, a dog dancing at her feet, and her head held high.

43

TWENTY-SECOND OF JUNE. Evening.

Dear diary,

You are my dearest and nearest confidant. I have so much on my mind today, it's now or never. And I just have to say this once and for all. I'm no worse than anyone else. Do you understand what I'm saying? But I was put to an impossible test, and even though I'm strong, it was just too much. The thing is Tommy dragged me down into the mud, and suddenly I was just the girl up at Granfoss with a disabled son. You know how people talk, it's unbearable. And it was definitely not what I'd planned for my life. What I'm writing now is really important, because it's the truth, and my case is coming up in only two days. I have to face the fact that I might be convicted. I just hope I can get away with a fine! Because then Dad could pay it and everything would finally be over for good. The way things are now, I might be convicted of negligence and moving the body, because I moved him from the bathtub to the pond. The inspector explained it all to me, and it doesn't sound good. I dreamed about death all through the long winter. He's sticking to me like a shadow and disturbs my sleep. Sits on the rug beside the bed baring his teeth.

On August 10, I ran a full bath and poured in lots of bubble bath, so the bubbles were almost over the edge. Because Tommy loved soap bubbles and I so wanted to be good and kind. You have to believe me. Tommy was being so difficult that day. Maybe he wasn't feeling well, what do I know? He was whining and complaining and didn't want anything, didn't want to be held or washed. He hit me with his little fists and tried to get me to go away. And I hate being rejected when I'm trying to be nice, I guess everyone does. I can only say I'm sorry, I really, really am. Because I just got so angry, you have to forgive me, dear diary. I am who I am, and children with Down syndrome are like that, they're difficult and obstinate and insistent. If there's something they don't want to do, they're impossible. I tried to force him, but he wouldn't be forced. It was like banging my head against a brick wall. I was on my knees beside the bathtub, holding him up with my left arm and trying to wash him with my right. I did look after him since he was the boy I'd been given, but I had the most terrible thoughts, that I had a child who wasn't normal, who had things wrong with him. I was sitting on the floor with a retard, and I didn't deserve it. I mean, what had I done? I hadn't broken any rules, I hadn't done anything to deserve being so unlucky. They say that everyone is worth the same. But that's not true, because there are idiots and they take up a lot of space and time. They're a burden to the rest of us. Is there anyone who has a child with Down syndrome who can put their hand on their heart and say that they hadn't hoped for something else? When they told me in the maternity ward, I wanted to scream. But I kept myself together for Dad's sake, and for Nicolai, obviously. He was in shock as well, even though he never admitted it. But he did take it better than me, I'll give him that, thanks to his cautious nature—in fact, he was almost a coward. His emotions never really came to the surface. He just moped around, and that's not healthy. So we took our slow, listless baby home with us. We took him home with heavy hearts. We had no choice, he was what we got. And we couldn't hand him back and say that we'd changed our minds. But oh, if only we could have done that! It would have been a joy, instead of all the sorrow and rage, bitterness and desperation. Family and friends came flocking to see the new baby, and I was so embarrassed, because they could see something was wrong. They could tell by his eyes that he wasn't normal. There were no delighted exclamations and I couldn't handle it. I just wanted to hide my face in shame because I was so embarrassed. And then they didn't know what to say, and it was all so awkward. I balled my hands and ground my teeth. My cheeks burned with humiliation. I thought about all these things as I sat there by the bathtub, with my difficult, soapy, slippery child in my hands.

I'm not bad! But I've always been impulsive and I just boiled over with rage and frustration. So I grabbed both his ankles and dragged him under. It happened on the spur of the moment. I want to say something really important here. I never once thought of killing him. I needed to vent my frustration, stop the whining and complaining that were getting on my nerves. There's nothing worse than a child screaming. It drives you mad, makes you feel like your head's going to explode. So I pulled him under. Within a few seconds he was hysterical. He flailed around with his hands and swallowed loads of water. Then I let go of his ankles and pushed him down with both hands, right to the bottom of the bathtub. I held him there until he started to spasm. Then I thought it was maybe enough, and gradually became myself again. And of course I regretted what I'd done, but it was too late, because he'd stopped fighting and in the space of about a minute he was limp and lifeless. But it took longer than I thought. The adrenaline made my heart pound and my mouth dry. I clenched my teeth, it wasn't easy. No matter what people might think if they'd seen me then, I didn't kill Tommy with a light heart. And

I don't want it to be said that I killed him with malicious fore-thought. It wasn't cold-blooded murder, because my blood has never boiled as it did that day in August. After a while he just lay there absolutely still at the bottom of the bathtub, with no more life in his eyes. The irises were dull, like milky glass. I almost didn't recognize him. He wasn't the Tommy I had given birth to anymore, just a cold, white, and wet unfamiliar little carcass. He'd thrown up and had foam around his mouth, and that's when it started to dawn on me what I'd done. I hadn't planned it, I'm not evil. I just wanted something different from Tommy, I didn't want all the shame. All the struggle. But then I had to find a way out of it. I had to give a more logical explanation, because sitting there on the floor I realized I had a major problem. I was sitting there with a dead baby and I needed an explanation. Which was why I told the first story that he'd managed to get down to the pond on his own two feet. And then because he was so eager, he'd gone out onto the jetty. Yes, I thought, of course that's what happened, and people would just have to believe it. After all, I always get my way, so I was used to it. I sat there for a while and listened but couldn't hear anything from the cellar, where Nicolai was busy with his bikes as usual. So I lifted Tommy up and carried him down to the pond. I walked through the grass with his little body in my arms. I stood out at the end of the jetty and looked at the black water with tears stinging my eyes. And, glancing quickly to the left and right, I threw him in. He was gone within seconds, sank like lead in the dark water. Just so you know, dear diary, I'm not without feelings, and I hadn't expected the police to catch me. So I had to change my story halfway. And I've done what I can just to get through this. I'm going to be a mother, after all, I've got responsibilities. I'm finally going to have another baby. It doesn't matter that Anders isn't too happy about it. I don't care about things like that, and in any case I decide over my life.

This is the whole and full truth.

And now I want to stop being plagued by these horrible dreams.

Go away, death, go away!

Granfoss, June 22, Carmen Cesilie Zita, on my honor.

44

TWENTY-THIRD OF JUNE. Midsummer's Eve, morning.

He called to her to see if she had any garbage. He had a couple
of boxes out in the hall and wanted to drive down to Stranda to
put them on the Midsummer bonfire. Carmen looked up from the
paper and saw his red curls, a shock of newly polished copper.
Anders looked nothing like Nicolai. He was much more muscu-
lar, with broad shoulders and big hands, and a jaw that indicated
strength and stamina. But she could still wrap him around her little finger, as she normally did with boys.

"What have you got in the boxes?" she asked.

She folded the newspaper and put it down.

"Old schoolbooks," he said hastily. "I found them down in the
cellar. And some old papers, I've tidied it all up, the drawers and
cupboards. I did it while you were sleeping. How are you? Are
you feeling better? I feel so helpless when you collapse like that.
You're not taking your medicine regularly, I know. Anyway, I'm
going to drive down to Stranda and throw all this on the fire. Papers shouldn't be thrown in the garbage, they should be burned;
don't you agree?"

"Yes," Carmen said. "I agree. Do you want me to come and
help?"

He shook his head. "No, I can do it myself. Don't worry. I won't be long. And you shouldn't be carrying anything in your condition."

She got up from the chair and went over to him. He kissed her gently on the cheek, because he couldn't get enough of her almost silky golden skin. He had snatched her from under the noses of a pack of flirting boys and he was proud of it. No matter where they went, her beauty drew attention. Young or not, Carmen was a catch and he would never find anything like her anywhere in the world. Nothing as beautiful as his angel with the white hair.

"Let's go out to eat tonight," he said. "It's so warm. I can't bear slaving over a hot stove in this weather." Carmen agreed. Her hands and feet were swollen and her head felt heavy. The beginning of a headache was whirring at her temples. He carried the boxes of books and papers out to the car and drove through the gate. Zita had put up a fence, which shone newly painted in the summer sun. A white fence now protected the old house. The pond was still there like a glittering black mirror, and it gnawed at her, making her irritable and annoyed. The whole thing had disrupted her orderly life. Damn, she thought, dammit! She calmed herself down and stroked her stomach. Life went on and she was in a good mood, even with the case pending. She was going to fight for her life. She would fight for her freedom with tooth and claw. Because she deserved it, at least that was how she saw it. She went out onto the step and waved. The dog jumped and danced beside her, barking happily into the clear air. Anders, she thought and smiled, my darling Anders. It's the two of us now, and our baby will be healthy.

Then she went in again with a growing unease because she hadn't looked to see what was in the boxes. She hadn't checked to see what he was throwing out. And now it was too late; the car had already disappeared around the bend, and the papers would soon be thrown on a bonfire to burn. She decided to write a last diary entry. So she went back into the living room, pulled out the bottom drawer in the desk, and started to look through it frantically. And as she rummaged, she got more and more agitated and her cheeks flushed. Because that was where she always kept her diary.

45

MIDSUMMER'S EVE, EVENING.

From here on in, the evenings and nights got longer and the days shorter. But for now, there was a beautiful light blue in the evening and a transparent dark at night, with fluttering, paper-thin moths dancing around the lights. The odd enthusiastic fly or an irritated wasp banged against the windowpane in search of something sweet.

It was the evening before the court case. Sejer drove up to Møller Church and wandered down the narrow paved path into the churchyard. His steps echoed in the stillness. Everything was green and growing, a promise of what lay in wait during summer's lush fruitfulness. Long, light, happy days. He wandered around for a short while before going to Tommy and Nicolai's graves, and then stood there for a moment as he mulled over what had happened. The sight of the two stones made him melancholy. In a way, they were together again, these two sorry souls, as they rested side by side. Both stones were covered in creeping ivy. If only I could find some irrefutable evidence, Sejer thought. Could she really have killed him with intent? As it stood, he needed proof. Something that he could lay on the table in court, something that was worth more than a feeling. From experience, he knew that his intuition was very well developed, and he had allowed himself to be guided many a time in situations where there was a glaring lack of technical evidence. If nothing else, it was an aid, a valuable supplement to knowledge. But he couldn't convince the state prosecutor with a feeling. It was laughably easy to be miserable, he thought, but you have to fight for happiness. Perhaps that was precisely what Carmen Zita had done. Catastrophe had struck, but she simply clenched her teeth and denied it all. No matter what, she'd kept her head above water. He thought about the past year and processed it into something he could understand. He drew comfort from it as he stood there, deep in thought, in the middle of Møller churchyard, surrounded by the dead. Well, I can't always have it my way. In this case, I'm not going to win. And I just have to accept the judgment, whatever it is. He steeled himself and then turned and went back to the car where Frank was lying in the back seat asleep, his wrinkled head on his paws. So, a quick walk at Stranda and then home. He started the car and swung out onto the road, his mind still caught up with tomorrow's court case. He remembered Nicolai's words from that last night. You mustn't believe a word of what Carmen tells you.

Lots of people had gathered wood for the Midsummer bonfire, which was bigger than ever before. A huge collapsed tower down by the water, it was a glorious mix of old broken pallets, cardboard boxes, and wood. A bed base, a stool and a wooden chair, boxes, cartons, and old packaging. People had also rummaged around in search of hidden treasures. It was a great midden of garbage and junk. Soon the flames would be leaping and the smell of burning would sear people's nostrils. Sparks would dance like shooting stars up into the dark blue night, while people stood around the fire with gleaming eyes and glowing cheeks. Sejer walked along the water, throwing a stick every now and then. Frank immediately scampered off to bring it back. After a while the dog got bored of this and started to investigate the bonfire. He sniffed around the pile of junk and eventually found his trophy for the day, a beautiful small notebook with a red cover. He carried it over to his master and dropped it at his feet, inordinately proud.